William Cotter Wilson

Poems of two worlds, containing the life and adventures of Santa Claus

William Cotter Wilson

Poems of two worlds, containing the life and adventures of Santa Claus

ISBN/EAN: 9783337242213

Printed in Europe, USA, Canada, Australia, Japan

Cover: Foto ©Andreas Hilbeck / pixelio.de

More available books at **www.hansebooks.com**

POEMS OF TWO WORLDS

CONTAINING

THE LIFE AND ADVENTURES OF SANTA CLAUS (An
Allegory), OO-LA-ITA (A Legend of Minnesota),
AND OTHER HISTORICAL, LEGENDARY,
ALLEGORICAL, HUMOROUS, MORAL
AND SPIRITUAL POEMS

BY WILLIAM COTTER WILSON

ILLUSTRATED BY ARTHUR CREIGHTON
AND TEACHENOR & BARTBERGER

PUBLISHED BY
H. T. WRIGHT
KANSAS CITY, MO.

List of Illustrations.

The reproductions of old cuts and zinc etchings by Carlton, Cops & Co.,
Kansas City, Mo.

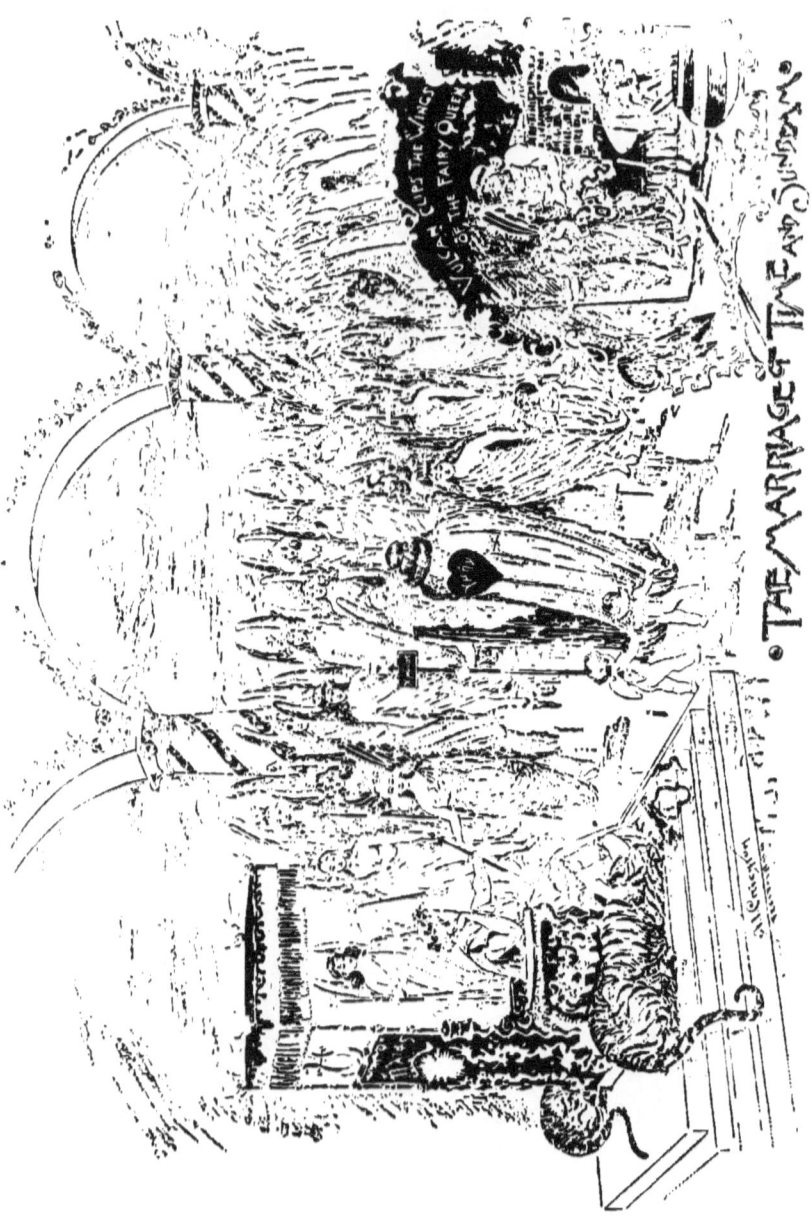

● THE MARRIAGE OF TIME AND SUNBEAM ●

"Here in my celestial home has earth's first nuptial knot been tied,
From out my courts shall worlds unknown the deathless universe divide."

DISGUISED ACROSTICS.

AMONG the following poems will be found many curiosities
of literature in the form of disguised acrostics. Being
known among my friends as an expert in acrostic writing,
most of them, if time permitted while I was visiting, would
suggest my writing something for them. Thus it is that many
of my poems contain the names of persons which would not be
discovered, though the poems were read for years; hence I here
append a list of acrostics with names attached. Many of these
are double acrostics, the first letters of alternate lines giving the
names of two persons, as, for instance, in the poem on page 57,
"My Childhood's Home." In this poem will be found the names
of a father and daughter, who were friends of mine. By reading
downward the alternate lines, beginning at top, the proper name,
Charles Rivers Brooke will be seen; then begin at first letter of
second line, read down alternately, and the name Alice Rivers
Brooke will be spelled out. In this way twenty of the poems have
names of persons disguised in the text. In some instances double
acrostics, as in the above example. In others, the name of one
person only; in such instances the first letter of every line, when
read downward, will give the name of the person for whom the
acrostic was written. A laughable illustration of how jealousy
will prompt to falsehood, will be found on page 122, entitled "An
Admonition." The text of note appended to poem will explain
itself. Poems of the character indicated will be found as follows:

SINGLE ACROSTICS.

DOUBLE ACROSTICS.

Then they a solemn contract drew, and Santa Claus affixed his name.

See page 19.

PREFACE.

COLERIDGE says, "Poetry has been to me its own exceeding great reward. It has given me the habit of wishing to discover the good and beautiful in all that meets and surrounds me." This expresses my own views and feelings so completely that I am glad to quote it. I have not only courted the Muse, but she has also courted me. From my earliest boyhood I was followed by an irresistible desire to express myself in verse. Many has been the time when some one who had incurred my displeasure, was made to feel the irony and ridicule of a couplet or verse that came to me as a weapon of defense or aggression as the exigency of the case seemed to demand. But my effusions were not all of that character. I was keenly sensitive to kindness and the loving side of my friends, and these formed better subjects for my pen than the insults, fancied or real, from my enemies. Nature, with her myriad charms in sea and sky, meadow and woodland, enraptured and fascinated me. And although something more than half a century has passed over me, I still find that the "world is full of beauty" to which I regret to say, the mass of mankind are as yet sadly blind. From time to time, I have given vent, in varied measure, to my emotions and ideality, and in some instances these have found their way into the columns of the literary journals of the day. I have frequently, I may say very frequently, been urged by friends to collect and publish in book form these numerous productions. The idea was by no means distasteful to me. But my profession, as an electrician, has made such unremitting and arduous demands upon my time that I have not found it possible, till within the last year, to carry out my own wish and comply with the desire of my friends. The volume is now, for the first time, given to the public. For its appearance I have no apologies to offer. In the language of Byron, "What is writ, is writ; would it were worthier."

The title, "POEMS OF TWO WORLDS," was selected, first, because some of the productions were written in the old world of Europe, and others in the new world of America. And next, because in accord with my belief in a future existence, I desire that my productions should not only serve a good purpose in this mundane sphere, but also point and lead to a higher, a grander and brighter life beyond. No one, I think, can justly complain of a want of poetic justice or moral tendency in what is herein placed before the reader. While I have on the one hand, written for the present hour, I have on the other, kept the great future steadily in contemplation.

Amongst the poems will be found several acrostics, and though these were written to please friends, yet it is hoped that apart from this motive they will be found to be of sufficient merit to justify their publication. It should also be observed that there are some acrostics that are marked as such, while others that are of an acrostic character are not so distinguished by their headlines.

There is one poem, the subject of which, so far as known, has never been treated of by any previous writer. I refer to "The Birth and Adventures of Santa Claus." While it is largely of an imaginative character, yet it is believed to be of that kind that will find favor not only amongst children, but also with other and maturer minds.

The Indian stories, of which there are two, are founded on history and tradition. In their preparation no greater license is indulged in than what is usually accorded to poetic productions. The reader will observe that I have in this volume treated on many subjects, ranging from the ridiculous to the sublime, from the grave to the gay, and it is kindly believed that their perusal will serve not only to brighten many an hour, but will also tend to create in the reader the habit spoken of by Coleridge "of wishing to discover the good and beautiful" in all that surrounds them.

                                    WM. COTTER WILSON.

POEMS OF TWO WORLDS.

SELF-ENLIGHTENED INTEREST.

WHY call this world a wilderness of woe ?
  Why speak of bleeding hearts and silent griefs ?
The tomb was never made for memory,
Yet, ne'er forgetting, we should ere forgive ;
Nor should the errors of our friends or foes
Absorb the dews and sunlight of the skies
To grow and keep afresh the wounds they made ;
But rather should we mark the hand of God
In all that is, for purpose wise and true.
All life at best is but a mystery,
And though ten million forms present themselves,
And each portray their separate cares and joys,
All by their acts proclaim a selfish end.
Hope is the heritage of every life,
Up from the monad, in insensuous soil,
To man, the proud expression of our God.
The truth is God ; and man that truth reveals
In all that he hath privilege to sway.
Our merchants yield to kings and potentates,
To them, in turn, the toiling mass succumbs—
And thus the gamut of our lives is run,
While self enlightened interest rules the whole.
Eternal food, in matter men may view,
Each atom, dead till force their forms unite,
Then up from seeming lifeless nothingness
A thinking, moving, generating form,
Perpetuates its kind eternally.
Herein the self-hood of insensuous things
Declares the fittest only shall survive ;
There is no death, nor can a thing be lost :

The microscopic wing that flits through space
Between the mobile atoms of the air
Bears up the cruder bulk, that pendant hangs,
And in its trunk the procreative germs
Mingle unseen, and yet these growths proclaim
The selfish right to live, and devastate
Our cherished homes, by sickness and disease.
Nothing is lost, what is must ever be;
We watch the foliage of our forest trees
And mark the varied tints and forms displayed,
But when brown Autumn seres their changeful dress
We oft in solemn tones pronounce them dead.
The very perfumes that regale our sense
May be restored through rock, or soil, or stream.
Therefore it is that Life can never die,
The deathless Soul of things must ever be.
To grant a God, is but to grant the Law,
And Law in God can ne'er be deemed to err,
What is is right, though interest demur.
For God could not be God, if Law could change;
If souls were born, such souls could change and die;
Soul is unborn, and God, the Soul of things,
Moves in and is a part of everything,
And all we know is but a part of God.
But Law is selfish and maintains its rights,
It moulds and keeps in form its separate shapes
In stone and plant and animated life;
One atom more or less of oxygen,
The thing called water, would itself destroy,
And chaos in its own small world would reign.
Thus all protection points to selfishness,
And self-enlightened interest the right of man.

A CRITIC CRITICISED.

[Written on reading an article on "Poetry and Rhyme," by James McCarroll
an American poet.]

O SHADE of Chaucer, aid my drooping pen,
　　And poise it equal to thy magic might,
For harsh McCarroll sits with journal men,
　　And from their sanctum would the poets fright.
And thou, O Spenser, while thy spirit lives,
　　Aid me to follow in thy rhythmic path;
For here I wander where the critic gives
　　His law of numbers in unmeasured wrath.
"As thick as berries on the upland moor,"
　　So says our critic, are the poets found ;
Nor does he wonder that each effort's poor,
　　While high-placed authors spread their errors round.
And yet 'tis pleasing, when he reasons thus,
　　With us poor dabblers in the measured page,
Nor need we tremble at the exodus,
　　As all must travel the allotted stage.
If by his dictum men like Milton sink
　　Down to the limbo of the tuneless bard,
And Gray be censured for one shattered link .
　　In his grand epic on the sacred sward ;
And our loved Byron, who with matchless skill
　　Now rose to fury, now to pity fell,
Though more than callous, yet his pages fill
　　The cup of mercy, while his pæons swell ;
Yet he the master of our English verse,
　　Whose lines majestic stood on every tongue,
And by his powers, and in his language terse,
　　Back to his critics all their venom flung.
And though long buried, must we listen yet
　　To one more critic of his rhythmic skill,
And all his beauties, all his loves forget,
　　And all the pictures that our fancies fill?

—2

Our critic renders to our Wordsworth fame,
  In one good quatrain shows his structure well;
But round the many piles the seething flame,
  And all would harrow with his rhythmic knell.
Shall bards be governed by a jingling rhyme,
  And all the beauties of the poet's soul
Be by his dictum deemed a lettered crime
  That must "be prisoned" round his mental pole?
But Carroll's raving and his rhythmic lore,
  His line of music where his jingles swing,
The bard of spirit o'er them both will soar,
  And e'en "though censured" in blank numbers sing.

THE SAVIOUR STANDS BY.

A STORM-TOSSED ship on the Southern Sea
    Was driven before the wind,
And the billows danced in their wildest glee,
  While the rifted rocks they climbed.

The proud ship stood like a knight at bay
  When faced by his foeman's steel,
Then parried the waves and bounded away
  Till the sunbeams lit her keel.

She soared like a bird on the swelling tide,
  And then came the deafening shock;
She had fought the fight with peerless pride,
  But sank on the surf-bound rock.

A tattered flag from the mizzen top,
  A boom from the signal gun,
Now bade a ship on her course to stop,
  And straight for the wreck to run.

The captain stood for the treacherous coast,
　　But it baffled his skill to try;
He did his all, it was his most,
　　To stand for the wrecked ones by.

He shoufed high o'er the billow's roar,
　　"Quick, quick, or all is done!
I'll wait the freight of the boats you lower,
　　But I cannot near you come."

Now bearing on o'er the battling waves
　　Were the freighted life-boats seen,
While the captain's heart for each one craves
　　Now life from the dying scene.

They climbed the side of the waiting ship,
　　And safe on her deck were found;
And the words, "Stand by!" from the captain's lips,
　　Echoed their welcome sound.

Now sinner know, like a ship at sea
　　Is the life you daily lead;
And the billows of sin are surrounding thee
　　While guilt is its written creed.

Though ye proudly stand with a knightly air,
　　And laugh at his demon call,
The sin-fiend seeks with a miser's care
　　Whate'er to his lot may fall.

He breathes on the world his upas breath,
　　And poisons the cloistered cell;
The lisping child and the aged at death
　　Are hushed by his venomed spell.

Though cast adrift on the shores of sin,
　　And left on the rocks to die,
The Saviour's voice o'er the billow's din
　　Is echoing, "I am by!"

A PRAYER.

A lmighty God! who o'er the world's expanse
N ow sits enthron'd in all thy majesty,
D escend and aid me in my reverence;
R eveal to me through Nature's eloquence
E arth's undiscovered mystic potencies,
W hich e'er as now hath ruled humanity.

G ive me, O God! to know thy wondrous will,
E nough of wisdom to conceive the agencies,
M atured by time, which now the world enwraps
M idst all the "foibles" of philosophers.
I f men dare strive against my conscious faith,
L ead me from out their creed's intricacies,
L est I should thoughtlessly destroy my friend.

[The above acrostic was written for Andrew Gemmill, who was a foster
brother of Robert Dale Owen, the founder of New Harmony and the writer
of the "Foot Falls on the Boundary of Another World," and a particular
friend of the author.]

PERJURY.

J USTICE sits paralyzed whene'er thy venomed tongue
    Attempts the disclosure of any social act;
Mercy is ever blind where'er thy mantle's hung—
    E'en Pity shrinks aback when thou relat'st a fact—
So seeming good and true, outside thy treachery.

Revolting, fiendish scourge, blaster of happiness,
    Oh, why did God allow thy entry in the world?
Born of rancoring discord, dost thou thus express
    Envy and enmity that thou from heaven was hurled,
Resenting o'er that fall from God's high sanctuary?

Thought, Reason, Peace and Love, in all their bright
        array,
Stand silent and appalled at thy vile utterances.
O'er all the moving world, where thou thy arts display,
Nature shrinks back abashed, like blackened night from
        day.

AN ODE TO MY ALBUM.

HAIL! hallowed tome! Thy casket leaves, all hail!
Thou art to me an open sepulchre !
Within thy walls I lay my cherished friends,
And gaze anon upon each absent face,
Enmirrored there by photographic art.
Each mute, lone face enthralls my soul,
And backward through the labyrinths of time
My memories glide o'er scenes of hope and care.
My schoolmates first, amidst the silent band,
Sweet childhood days, enrapturing thoughts inspire !
Maturer years, when love's first fires did burn,
Are here recalled with all the vivid scenes
Thro' which I passed, till manhood's years were reached;
Here, then, began the real and earnest life,
When many of the faces here portrayed
In all the vigor of their manhood lived.
Some early sought the ne'er returning bourne,
While others left through stranger lands to roam ;
But now, remaining as my constant friends,
Are some whose faithful pictures here I scan.
My father dead yet seems to live again,
The while I look upon his portrait now.
My mother, too, upon whose knee I sat,
She who, through life a beacon and a guide,
Taught me to know my duties to the world,
But she no more can mingle in the throng
Of busy mortals in the marts of trade,
And yet, I feel her spirit at my side,
While I upon her silent picture gaze.
Brothers and sisters, friends and kindred, too,
Gather in spirit, like flocks within a fold.
Dear album, thou a temple art to me,
In which I worship with the living dead !

SIGHS AND TEARS.

OH, how sweet's the release of a sigh,
    And the solace which follows a tear,
When the heart with emotion beats high,
    If in anguish or sorrow or fear!

He who painted the blush on the rose,
    And gave to the violet perfume,
Did the stars in the heavens dispose,
    And created our hope through the tomb.

We are but a few atoms at best,
    Yet God hath his attributes given,
With the sigh and the tear his behest
    On earth to prepare us for heaven.

Oh, then let not the thoughtless e'er say
    That 'tis folly to weep or to sigh,
But remember 'tis Nature's own way
    The fountains of sorrow to dry.

TO THE OLD YEAR.

WIPE from his beard the crystal breath, the frosty air
        hath chill'd,
And gently close the drooping lids, the scenes of life hath
        still'd;
Straighten the limbs and smooth the brow and kiss the pal-
        lid cheek,
And lay him softly on the bier, for he no more can speak.

'Tis true the old man's dead to-night; he whom we know so
        well,
And yet it seems but yesterday, when first the sunlight fell
Upon the head of him who now, in whiten'd locks lies low,
And leaves behind but memories, of love and peace and woe.

To a Dead Child.

AN ACROSTIC.

Round our hearts, like tender vinelets trailing o'er the sturdy
oak,
Upward looking for protection, thine eyes a voiceless language spoke.
Sunlit meteors, from their orbits, pierced the shadows of our
home;
Such the eyes that beamed upon us, they our sorrows would
atone.
Entered scarcely on the pathway that would lead thee through
the world,
Like a lamb from shepherd straying, we have missed thee
from the fold.
Light of heaven, guide thee homeward, upward through the
streets of gold.

Hearts and hands will still surround thee, spirit voices sing
to thee.
And thy friends will give thee welcome, sailing o'er the jasper sea.
Music, through the halls supernal, echoing back from heav-
en's dome,
Makes thy presence here among us feel a jointure in thy
home.
Entered on thy endless journey through the beauties of the
spheres,
Russell, deathless child of spirit, thou canst come and dry
our tears.

[The above acrostic was written for the album of Hon. Mr. Hammer,
of Chicago, whose child, his only son, was, after a few hours' illness, taken
from him almost without warning.]

BEAUTIFUL EYES.

I WALK'D through the meadows at the dawn of the day,
  When the sun o'er the hill-tops beglistened the dew,
While the scent of the flowers, and the odors of May,
  Told the story of Springtime in language anew.

I watched every droplet on the tall nodding grass,
  Swaying backward and forward, controlling each blade,
While nature seem'd lured by each spherical glass,
  And the soft fanning zephyrs roll'd on through the glade.

Helena, my school mate, had stole from her room
  Unchallenged, to wander with me at the dawn;
Her lessons unheeded, uncar'd for the doom
  Which her hard-hearted school-dame around her had
    drawn.

When she look'd up to me, with her beautiful eyes,
  Surpassing the dewdrops which stood at our feet,
Aurora-wrapt brightness unfolded the prize,
  Which shadowed the blossoms with graces replete.

We plighted our troth on that early spring morn,
  And Cupid and Hymen the nuptial knot tied.
Though the hyssop would grow, and the rose have its thorn,
  I never regret that I made her my bride.

The brightness of childhood now reigns in her face,
  And the charms of her womanhood dwell on her brow,
Her form is as perfect, and as pleasing her grace
  As when on th' May morning I pledged her my vow.

'Twas nature in childhood, 'twas nature in youth,
  'Twas nature when womanhood claimed me her own,
'Twas nature preserved her, 'twas nature, forsooth,
  Which now in the seventies dares to atone.

Disease may be rampant, but Nature stands by,
  And shouts to the echo throughout her domain;
There is naught in the heavens, the earth or the sky
  But ever responds to her magic refrain.

SOLILOQUY ON DUST.

[This poem was written extempore at the request of a friend, on taking the dust from a shelf in a room and holding the particles on his finger.]

INCONGRUOUS mass!
Unfashioned, dull and unadorned;
The unsensed atoms of thy bulk
Man's searching wisdom may divine.
Not so the Power which permeates
The whole with hidden laws;
These man doth not, nor can he understand,
Unless some power as yet unknown
Unveils the secret springs of life
    And shows the cause.

    Say, what is life?
Ye sage philosophers who strive
To search through matter for its laws;
Can ye define or render clear
The power which gives it motion?
Or doth some common barrier keep
Ye and the duller mortals back,
In one commingled, listless throng,
Each struck with awe the while ye gaze
    On life's trite forms?

    'Tis well to know
The action of dissimilar things;
The various gases that assume
A given form, by given parts conjoined.
Such knowledge aids us in our search,
And wisely used, directs our thoughts
To that great cause of life and being
Which from eternity hath been
The motive power and sole support
    Of this our world.

    But take the dust
From off some marble portico,
'Neath which the haughty purse-proud tread,

Or, from some peasant's crumbled cot,
Collect the dull and dingy mass
That time hath packed beneath the eaves;
This, laid in heaps, will germinate;
Such varied forms of life assume,
Defying all the arts of man
      To trace the cause.

    Who hath not watched
A sunbeam dazzling in the shade,
Wherein a countless host display
The power of matter to assume
A form invisible to man.
Which, but for the sun's effulgence
Would to the unlettered yet remain
A hazy phantom of the mind,
And human speech would fail to give
      An explanation.

    Yet thou, proud man,
With all thy wondrous parts conjoined;
Thy quick conception and thy speech,
Thy brain's vast empire and the train
Of wonder-working faculties
With which thou art alone endowed,
By nature set upon the world
The living prototype of power;
Yet thou wert dust, and must return
      To dust again.

    Look back through time
And try to print upon your brain
The virgin world's chaotic mode,
When e'en the essence of your lives
As yet had not begun to be,
And say canst thou conceive a Form
Somewhere existent, with the power
To call to being all forms of life
Which now the universe display?
When thus conceived, but not till then
      Can ye believe in God.

THE REVERIE OF THE IRISH EMIGRANT.

[A description of the country between Brayhead and Glendalough. Here
it was that Moore wrote the most of his Irish Melodies.]

SWEET home of my childhood, dear sylphs of the glen,
    Loved sprites of the Dargle, I court ye again !
O, lead me in spirit thy mountains among,
Tho' far from the fir-crowned coverts of song.
In the wilds of Columbia, 'midst mountains of snow,
An alien I roam, where her wild torrents flow ;
Still the silver-tipped waters of Powerscourt vale
And the scenes of my childhood loom up through the gale ;
The streams of the Vartry purling on the town,
Where the brown-heather'd mountains of Wicklow look
    down
On my loved Enniskerry, by the rock-severed Scalp,
Which pales in its beauty the snow-covered Alp.
When the crimson-faced sun o'er the Sugarloaf fell,
And nature in silence reigned over the dell,
On its evergreen hillocks I would stay me to rest,
With the cheek of my Maggie, love, laid on my breast,
While away in the distance the headland of Bray,
Looking o'er the wild ocean, our thoughts would betray,
And pictures of freedom, of wealth and of ease,
Stript the glen of its beauties, our hopes to appease.
We talked of the joys in the land of the free,
And pictured in fancy our home as 'twould be ;
But fate, th' cruel guardian, kept watch at my side,
And robb'd me of Maggie, my hope and my pride ;
In the vale of Avoca they laid her to sleep,
And left me to wander alone o'er the deep ;
Far o'er the wide ocean, o'er mountain and plain,
I have sought me a home, but have sought it in vain ;
For where is the home without those whom we love?
O, where can we rest from our friendships removed?
Then let me go back to the Glen of the Downs,
To the sweet Dargle streams and Avoca's green mounds;

Let me watch the wild cataract over the fall,
And once more the days of my childhood recall;
Let me hear the sweet note of the skylark on high,
And the linnet's shrill song in the covert hard by;
Let me wander again through the Ballyman glen:
By the Scalp overshadowed, deep hidden from men;
Where the well of St. Kevin low nestling from view,
Was covered by tributes which pilgrims bestrew;
O, how well I remember when Maggie and I
Stopped to drink of its waters, all parching and dry;
When we split up our 'kerchiefs and swore to be true,
As our path by the suicide's grave did pursue.
When the remnants we hung on St. Kevin's ash tree,
We swore then forever ne'er parted to be,
And there by the bush-covered church in the glen,
We prayed to St. Kevin again and again.
The sombre-leaved holly in the vale of Glencree,
And the hills of Glencullen found pleasure for me,
While the sides of the Douce towering up to the sky,
Through its rock-channel surface the Dargle supply
With its silver-tipp'd waters that danced through the vale,
Scarce touched with the sunshine or brushed with the gale,
Through the sylvan retreats of the Dan and the Tay,
And to old Glendalough I would wander away.
Ah! bleak Massachusetts, I'll bid thee farewell,
And aback to my home in the hollybrook dell,
Where the evergreen, oaks and the cypress and yew
O'ershadow the ruins of Kilmacanague.
Through the dark narrow glade where the brooklet steals by;
The pass in the mountains towering up to the sky;
Where the Downs from the Sugarloaf, split by the stream,
Keep back by their shadows the sun's piercing beam,
There again I will roam at the dawn of the day,
And when labor is o'er through the valley I'll stray,
And feel myself blessed at the sight of the streams
Which enwrapt me with pleasure through life's early dreams.
Through the Delgany vales and the hills of Bellevue,
And the green parks of Tinna my walks I'll renew.
E'en now in my fancy that country I scan
From the Downs lofty mountain to the vale of Dunran,

Through the vista of time I look back on the day
When the stones in the brook of Glendaragh I lay,
Whereon I could step, as with pleasure I bore
My love o'er its waters to high Altadore ;
Though thirty long years with their changes I've seen,
The Hermitage still is as fresh in the scene
As when o'er its rough broken stones I would tread,
And the cloth for our picnic between them was spread,
When the sweet voice of Maggie re-echoed the dell
As it joined with the notes of the birds as they fell
On our ears from the cone-covered pines in the glade,
Till I felt as though Orpheus was hid in the shade ;
I'll leave thee, Columbia (my long foster home),
And back to green Erin again I will roam,
And there I will dwell until summoned from men,
To meet in the Heavens my Maggie again.

HOPE.

HOPE is the warrior's strength with which he wields his
sword ;
Hope will press the minstrel on to sound his harpsichord ;
Hope the weary seaman soothes in wreck, or storm or gale ;
Hope will urge the artist on, tho' first his work may fail ;
Hope the poet's pen will guide through satire, play, or song ;
Hope, it is the sculptor's rock to carve his figures from ;
Hope's the axletree of life, on which its car must sway ;
Hope once lost, our life must fail, and death must end our day.

LIFE AND MAGNETISM.

BENEATH our feet we crush at every tread
   The pregnant life-cells of a world unborn,
'Tis but by God-made law this world we know
Hath 'scaped destruction from the feet of time.
The glow-worm's lamp, the firefly's fitful spark,
The rainbow hues which deck the gad-fly's wing,
Are but the changing conformations of the dust
Moved into life by the magnet's subtle force.

Thus from the womb of earth unnumbered millions
     spring,
Each differing in their form, yet all imbued
With that same force which built the mastodon
And gives the spider its intelligence.
The woven cobwebs clinging to your walls,
The geometric cell of wasp or bee,
The matted chrysalis of the butterfly,
Are but the outcome of magnetic law.

Shut from yourselves the sunbeam's radiant light,
Prison your flowers in cloisters dank and dark ;
Nature would then her lamp of life bedim,
And our existence make a charnel-house.
The cells which form the network of our nerves
Are moved to motion by the self-same law
Which holds the planets to their orbits' course
And keeps this world from rushing into space.

IPHETONGA.

[The following poem pictures one of the most remarka .e incidents of American history. Hendric Hudson was employed by the government of Holland, to discover, if possible, "the northwest passage." It was in this endeavor he drifted along the shore of "Long Island." Allured by the wild grapes and plums growing along the fertile beach of far Rockaway and Carnarsie, he lowered his boats from his good ship, "Half Moon," and with his crew made for the shore. The Carnarsie and Rockaway Indians had watched from their wigwams the strange craft, as also the boats pulling for the shore, and wading out through the surf, met the strangers as they struck the beach. This was the beginning of American civilization.

"Iphetonga" was the name of an Indian princess, who, with her tribe, dwelt upon the bluffs opposite New York City, now known as "Brooklyn Heights," at whose feet runs the beautiful river "Manhattan," since named "The Hudson," in honor of its discoverer.]

IPHETONGA.

GONE and forever are the whoops of Carnarsie!
No more doth the brushwood conceal the dark foe;
No more do the Rockaways hunt through the cedars,
Which lined the broad beach stretching out to the sea.
Gone are the vineyards and the surf-sprinkled plum trees,
Which lured to Manhattan, young Hudson, the brave;
No more do we barter the skins of our Island,
As did the wild Indian who dwelt on our shores.
When the Half Moon bore down on the white sands of Coney,
The wild wolf was heard through the tall, pointed pines,
While out through the surf came the clamoring natives
To meet the brave crew as they rowed for the shore.
Their pow-wows they raised to the spirit of evil,
And offered the wampum surrounding their bodies,
For beads and for trinkets the white men presented,
And friendship cemented the hour of their landing.
Down through the decades hath passed the strange story
Which gave to the river surrounding Manhattan
A name that midst nations is spoken with pride;
And hailed as the conduit of ne'er dying freedom.
Columbus, the Spaniard, in the height of his prowess,
Ne'er dreamed that the fleets of the world would be anchored,

Breast deep on the waters which Hudson since named,
While up through Gowanus his Dutch ship was steered.
When they gazed on the woods of the high Iphetonga,
Which towered o'er the stream in the front of Manhattan
While paddled the savage his tree-formed canoe,
Fresh freighted with furs from the wolf and the beaver,
The glass beads of Amsterdam paid for the treasures,
For which the wild savage had toiled through the season,
Yet happy was he the bright gewgaws to gather,
And gave for the baubles the fruits of his labor.

    *   *   *   *   *   *   *   *   *

But changed is the scene since the advent of Hudson,
For the hands of the white man have leveled the woodlands,
And the dusky browed savage hath gone to his fathers
And left Iphetonga the queen of the ocean.
The wigwams were cleared for the homes of the white man,
The loom took the place of the bow and the arrow,
The ax and the adz then fashioned the timbers
And built the proud ships which were launched on our waters.
No more o'er the woodlands nor down by the river,
Where proud Iphetonga uplifted her head,
Do we hear the wild whoop of the red-painted Indian,
And the howl of the wolf in the forest is ended.
But up from the sea rose the white sands of Coney,
And gave us the Island, the pride of our country,
Where men of all nations can mingle for pleasure,
And pass the hot months midst the spray of its waters.
The rich and the lowly, the proud and the humble,
Send back to their fatherland tales of their sporting
On the banks of the ocean where Hudson first landed,
Far back in the decades among the wild savage.
How little we think, while we sport in the waters,
Of the terrible scenes which gave to the white man
The right to the Island from the savage Carnarsies.
Who fought to the death for the land of their fathers.

[Her Majesty's gun-boat, the Eurydice, was a ship of twelve guns, with a
crew of four hundred all told. She had been sent to cruise off the Islands of
Barbadoes, in the West Indies, and, through some accident, was lost sight of
for a long time, and many of the friends of the crew mourned them as lost,
when the news came to them and the government that she was safe, and on
the 24th of March, 1878, it being Sunday, the people on the Isle of Wight were
watching all day the lost ship's return, when at about 2 o'clock in the after-
noon, she was sighted off Ventnor and Bon Church Downs, sailing merrily
along with all sails full set, on her road to the Downs, which was her destination, being only about two hours' sail to her anchorage. The people on shore
could see the crew on deck waving their caps and handkerchiefs, while the
church bells of Bon Church could be heard on the deck of the ship. Amidst
all the joys of the home-coming of the ship and crew, a sudden squall blew
up, and the port-holes of the ship, being all open, admitted of the ingress of
water as she fell over on her side, and thus in ten minutes not a sign of the
ship was seen and only two persons survived to tell the tale of all the crew
on board. Marcus Hare was seen to cling to the side of the ship and went
down, never to rise again until God shall call him hence to that home where
billows never roll nor ships go down in sight of home. The author was inti-
mately acquainted with Fletcher, one of the survivors.]

THE LOSS OF THE EURYDICE.

HURRAH! hurrah! hurrah! we're home,
    Three hundred voices cried ;
And their merry shouts were echoed back
    Across the surging tide.
The proud ship danced like a neighing steed,
    As she tript each sunlit wave ;
And the golden gleams from Vecta's Hills
    Their silent welcome gave.

Now the terraced town of Ventnor rose
    All glorious on the scene ;
And the music of the Bon Church bells
    Swept o'er the village green ;
They had sighted the sound by Edgecombe Hill,
    And left Devonia behind ;
And Dorset's plains receded from view,
    As they leapt before the wind.

Then the Sabbath prayers were offered up,
    And the Sabbath psalms were sung ;
And every man now joined in praise
    To the Good and Holy One.

—3

"Ahoy, my lads! set every sail!"
   The captain proudly cried;
"With this fair wind, ere the sun is set,
   We shall safe at anchor ride."

Then every man of the watch on deck
   At his duty's post was found:
As the sheets swelled out with the rising wind
   And bore on the homeward bound;
The off-watch crew were writing below
   To sweethearts, parents and friends,
And tokens of love were scan'd anew,
   With many promised amends.

One saw his wife o'erpowered with joy,
   Come running adown the strand;
While another heard his sweetheart's voice
   And in fancy grasped her hand:
They knew the electric wires had told
   The news of their safe return,
And felt again their plighted troth
   Anew in their bosoms burn.

The sailor boy of the morning watch
   Had slept through the sunlit day;
But leapt with joy when told how short
   Was his time on board to stay:
He took from his breast the silken bag,
   Which his mother bade him wear,
And viewed with joy each separate lock:
   The locks of his sisters' hair.

Ah, this is Annie's auburn curl
   Which grew o'er her snowy brow:
And this is Jennie's chestnut lock
   Which I clipt it seems but now:
And this is mother's silvery hair
   Which father took to sea,
And wore it in this very bag.
   Till dying left it me.

And these the everlasting flowers,
   Which grew by the garden path,
Adown which my school-mate, Jane and I,
   Oft fled from the school-dame's wrath ;
But mother dear, and sisters too,
   I feel our meeting nigh,
When e'en the school-dame will forgive
   The wrongs of Jane and I.

Hark! hark! the boatswain's voice is heard,
   All hands are piped on deck;
Strike! strike! the topsails, lower the sheets,
   Or our good ship's a wreck ;
The gallant hands to the rigging flew
   In spite of the blinding squall;
And there they worked, as brave a band
   As ever obey'd a call.

'Twas all in vain; gaunt, giant death
   Had seized the unbending helm ;
And the storm fiend clung to the trembling ship
   The sailors to overwhelm.
There's no time to cut the pinnace free,
   There's no time the boats to lower ;
But each seaman fought with destiny
   In sight of his native shore.

Then the ship fell broadside on the waves
   While the sails dipp'd in the sea,
The drowning shrieks of that noble crew
   In a moment ceased to be.
Brave Marcus Hare was the last man seen,
   Alone on that sinking ship,
And calmly stood as she glided down
   Till the salt waves kiss'd his lip.

And the two survivors proudly tell
   Of the captain's noble mein,
As from the side of the Eurydice
   He gaz'd on the closing scene ;

And how he clung to his sinking ship
   Like a lover to his bride ;
And how like a sailor he had lived,
   And there, like a sailor, died.

May young Fletcher live to hear the tale
   Told by his grandson's child ;
How he and his comrade, Cuddiford,
   Bare up through that tempest wild ;
How, on that eventful Sunday eve,
   They rode on a sunlit foam,
When a blinding squall o'ertook the ship,
   Which sunk in the sight of home.

THE PHILOSOPHY OF LIFE.

THE star depths of empyrean space convey
      Between the moving atoms of the air
That subtle aura, floating from the sun,
Which moulds the germs of universal life.

The sun's volcanoes, belching forth their fires,
Through darkened space, on thro' our atmosphere,
Pour their magnetic ether on the earth,
Till life from dead inertia seems to spring.

But back of all a hand divine is seen,
And atheists' ravings melt to nothingness,
From whence or where the cause of earth and sky
Is not vouchsafed for puny man to know.

Parent of worlds, mother, or father—God,
We owe thee tribute, though we know thee not,
Thy handiwork throughout creation claims
Our homage for thy vast munificence.

DEATH'S PRIME MINISTER.

A TEMPERANCE ALLEGORY.

DEATH in his council chamber sat,
   Surrounded by a ghastly train
Of sordid lust, disease and vice,
   Crouched near his throne, in ling'ring pain.
The most detested fiend of hell
   Stood near the grisly Monarch's chair.
His name was Guilt; his putrid breath
   The pandemonium's atmosphere ;
While Conscience, fettered like a slave,
   Stood side by side with pale-eyed Fear,
Trembling, as the lightnings flashed
   Through murky panes and fetid air.
The Monarch, from his skull-built throne,
   With weird commanding, hollow voice
Spoke thus: My mandate, be it known,
   To decide the primate of my choice.
Delusion, who stood list'ning by,
   Was bid to guard the palace gate,
That he might usher to the throne
   Whoever came as candidate.
First, silent, hectic Asthma came,
   With shoulders bent and bated breath,
In words half-uttered, pressed his claim,
   For the proud Premiership of Death.
Then hobbled in on ashen stick,
   Plethoric Gout with bandaged limbs ;
While at his side his cousin stood,
   Rheumatic, with his hundred whims.
Then Colic, writhing in distress,
   With wild contortions fright the throng,
And showed, by frantic, wild grimace,
   How he could prostrate old and young.

Next, Cholera came with leaden face,
  And brow bedewed with clammy sweat,
And told how countless myriads,
  Through him alone, their doom had met.
Then lurid Fever forward pressed,
  In hurried accents thus began :
Most noble Liege, in me behold
  Thy faithful servant, scourge of man !
The various guises I assume
  Empowers me every home to reach,
And madness follows in my wake,
  And widens out my every breach.
Consumption next approached the King,
  With glassy eyes which pierced the gloom,
Then peering at the clamoring band,
  She smiling pointed to the tomb.
See! Here the tottering infant rests ;
  And here, the parents' hopeful youth,
And here, the bride but newly wed!
  Anon the bridegroom rests, forsooth!
With deep flushed face I oft decoy ;
  The guise of beauty bid them wear ;
So sure my aim, they all must fall,
  Though they for years evade my snare.
Thus, every claimant pressed his suit,
  And anxious waited the award,
And all was silent as the tomb ; —
  Not e'en a heaving breast was heard :
When from without, a reveling band
  And Bacchanalian songs were heard :
Then, fell each moment on the ear
  Some envious, vile, blasphemous word.
A woman, then, with head erect,
  Pacing through the aisles was seen ;
A vine-leaved crown her head bedecked, —
  A serpent in her hand was seen :
Licentious youths walked at her side,
  And wanton harlots led the choir,
While Clamour, following, did deride,
  And Anger vented forth his fire.

Beneath her scrutinizing gaze,
  The boastful claimants seemed to pall,
And thus she spoke, as on she pressed —
  "I am the mother of ye all!
Stand back! ye knaves, your king shall hear
  How I have always served the State,
Nor dare ye now to interfere
  Till I, my every claim relate :
Intemperance is the name I bear,
  I claim my birthright from the vine,
And millions, humbled in the dust,
  Found out too late what powers were mine.
I rear my castles everywhere,
  And every scheming art devise,
Till my insidious powers are known,
  To crush alike, the dull and wise!"
At once a gleam of pleasure passed
  Across the Monarch's grisly face,
And those who sat elate, before,
  With sorrowing hearts their steps retrace.
Death 'rose, and with a smothered smile,
  His hollowed voice the chamber rang:—
My Premier is Intemperance,
  And hath been since the world began!

[The following poem was written in the City of Waterford, Ireland, upon the occasion of a begging petition being sent around for money to purchase an estate for Prince Arthur, upon his marriage, and this while the Irish peasantry were starving for bread, and when the *habeas corpus* act was suspended in Ireland, and the author had to escape from Waterford to avoid arrest for sedition, or his fate would have been that of Davitt and others who were so unfairly treated at about the same time.]

AN IRISH APPEAL FOR A POOR PRINCE.

DUKE OF CONNAUGHT PRESENTATION.

The Lord Mayor begs to acknowledge the receipt of £49 0s 6d from Lord Listowel; £12 14s 6d from Mayor of Waterford; 2s 6d from Rev. S. Clarke, Kingstown; £1 from Major Leech, and £1 from David Arnott, Irish Times Office.

KIND Christian friends, who feel for others' woe,
  A Royal Prince would to the altar go—
But his poor dame, so sparsely fed and clad,
Can nothing give to help her soldier lad.
Then send around the hat to all who feel
An interest in this wooing Princeship's weal.
From Lee's green banks high up to Causeway head,
Let Charity her Christian bounties spread—
From Wicklow's hills to Galway's rugged plains
Collect the pence from labor's hard wrought gains ;
Bid landlords starve the tillers of the soil,
And crimp the wages of their daily toil,
That they may pile the blood-wrought lucre high—
The coffers thus of this young prince supply ;
Then set apart some dozen miles of land,
Where HE when wed may henceforth hold command—
Where he can keep to labour's market price,
And follow Darnly in his blood-bought vice—
Like Lord Tredeger teach them how to carve
The oatmeal cake, on which they cannot starve.
Eject some hundred tenants from their home,
And bid them wander houseless and alone.
Then give the proceeds to this Royal pair,
And consecrate the act in Christian prayer—
Medina's waters, back'd by Veeta's heights,
Where Osborne House in castle form delights,

Have lost their spell this Irish Duke to charm
Who fain for aye would lean on Erin's arm.
Ye loyal sons of Erin's "prosperous" Isle,
Who, hap'ly placed, ne'er heard of "landlord's guile!"
Where every rood of land from sea to sea
To rich and poor alike was ever free.
This Eden Isle, where want is "never known,"
Should surely find some succour for the throne.
Then give from out your ever "bounteous store,'
To aid this Prince, so noble—yet so poor.
Poor England gave, and so did Scotia, too,
To help this Prince seek out a home with you—
Though evil men with vile intent hath said
That Erin's sons are starving now for bread—
Who lack the means the wants of life to earn,
And misery's rampant—no matter where you turn.
Oatmeal so cheap, and river water free,
Men need not starve, nor talk of misery—
Ye loyal Mayors of every Irish town,
Yield ratepayers' cash, nor heed the starvelings' frown,
But flood the columns of the daily Press,
And advertise young Connaught's sore distress.
Heed not the wails of all that workhouse brood,
Who, sick and starving, clamor now for food.
But let them die if it be God's decree,
Good riddance, too, from such incumbrance free.
In one short year we spent on workhouse wine
What would have served an Alderman to dine,
A dozen Princes and the Royal suite,
And won a Knighthood for the civic treat.
We ought to do as did our friend St. Paul,
The civic magnate of Northampton Hall,
Who, when poor Wells, at sixty years of age,
Refused his aid, the workhouse to assuage,
From sixteen shillings, earned near every week,
He would not give his one-and-six per week—
So off to gaol, with felons he was led,
Handcuff'd and chain'd, to eat the prison bread.
This glorious law of Queen Victoria's reign
Should be enforced in Ireland once again—

Then freely give, with loyal and generous hand,
And young Prince Arthur welcome to our land—
A castellated dwelling now provide
Upon the banks of Shannon's crystal tide.
By tithes and taxes pay his yearly bill,
Tho' widows weep for starving children still—
Then think of all the honors you achieve,
When you the wants of this young Prince relieve—
Remember, too, that all must meet above,
And prince and peasant in one phalanx move.
What boots it then if starving men should wait
Without the halls, wherein in civic state,
As much is spent in Aldermanic cheer
As would provide a thousand for a year.
Then give it forth unto the thoughtless throng
That to this Prince our sympathies belong ;
That th' old adage we so long have known—
That charity should e'er begin at home—
May all be true where poor the poor provide,
But not where Princes seek a Royal bride.
In such a case we nothing have to do
But send the hat and satchel round to you.
And our success the better to insure,
The largest City Hall we must secure.
Of course the costs the rates will all defray,
Or we may lower the city sweepers' pay,
Or tell the nurses of each workhouse ward
That food is dear and times so very hard
That we must crimp the food and fuel supply,
Nor heed the want on't if the paupers die.
A glorious future then awaits our scheme,
When our loyal acts shall be the common theme,
And Lords and Commons in no distant day
May grant a knighthood as the royal pay,
And perhaps some day will recognize the fact,
Again suspend the Habeas Corpus Act,
To gag the mouths and freedom of our Isle,
Or place our patriots into dungeons vile.
What once has happened may perhaps occur again,
For Erin's history runs in such a vein.

All men are fools who boast the patriot's name,
And fools and rogues should all be served the same ;
The love of country and all such balderdash
Is best requited by the gaoler's lash —
For what is country and our friends at home
Against the love that we should bear the throne,
Which but for it the offices we hold
Could not be purchased by our surplus gold,
But brains instead would win the foremost place,
And fustian distance broadcloth in the race.
The stocks and shares that now our coffers fill
Would be divided at our workmen's will,
For they would teach that all their work and brains
Are worth as much as is our idle gains.
Have they not dared a certain price to lay
On every hour they work on any day?
And if we yield to dictates such as these,
Why we would need to earn our bread and cheese —
To walk out early through the frosts and snows,
With holes through elbows and through boots our toes ;
At breakfast time seek out some shelter near
To eat our bread and drink our water clear,
To let them keep the land they have improved,
And us abuse should they be e'er removed ;
With brooms and brushes soil our daughters' hands,
Which now are trained for Broadwood's dulcet strands
In fact, they'd teach that flesh and blood's the same
In aldermanic or through peasant's vein,
That plebeian blood is good as loyal blue,
And human nature all alike imbue.
Then give, my friends, this Royal Prince your aid,
And let all nonsense in the dust be laid,
And hear the Queen through Parliament declare
That Ireland found a castle for the pair
Who had by birth nor blood one single claim
But 'twas alone her confidence to gain —
Yes, tell the Queen that famine, want, despair,
Throughout our land is rampant everywhere,
In spite of which we ope'd our purses wide
To welcome Arthur and his Royal bride.

MY CARD TRAY.

MY card tray stood by the parlor door,
  Well filled with the scripts of ten long years;
I turned the mementoes o'er and o'er,
  Midst pleasure and pain and falling tears.

Each well remembered name I scanned,
  And paused anon midst heaving sighs
And fitful smiles, while through my hand
  The time-stained cards in turn would rise.

Annie Revere, my schoolmate friend,
  Left this upon her wedding day;
E'en now I see her hand extend
  As on that morn she went away.

But Annie, alas! her fate was sealed,
  For ere the sun its cycle sped
The muffled bell for my schoolmate peal'd,
  And the bride of a year we mourned her dead.

Here is Barney St. Clair, that dear old man
  Whose snow-white locks before my gaze —
Are as vivid as when to the gate I ran
  And welcomed him home in my childhood days.

But he is as young as at forty-five,
  And his hair is as full, and his eyes as bright
As when in my childhood glee I'd strive
  In blindman's buff to hide from sight.

[This was written after reading the remarkable story of a Mr. Cogman, who was a carpenter living in London. His daughter, Emily Cogman, had been in the London hospital, in the Whitechapel Road, for several months, suffering from consumption, and a few days before her death the doctors sent for Mr. Cogman and told him his daughter was convalescent and could with benefit to herself leave the hospital, she being very strong and in a fair way of ultimate recovery. Mr. Cogman thereupon caused a suite of rooms to be prepared for her, he being a widower and living alone. On the Saturday, midday, he was in the rooms preparing for her reception, when looking up from the carpet he saw his daughter come through the solid door without opening it. He became somewhat alarmed but rose to meet her only to find she had left. Thereupon he hurried off to the hospital and as he walked down the aisle of the ward in which his daughter had lain he saw in the distance his daughter rise from the bed in the dress she had worn in the room an hour before, and which was the one she had worn when she first went to the hospital. As she floated towards the ceiling she held out her arms, seeming to catch the longing look of her father, and addressed him this farewell: "Father, fare thee well; think of me when I am there." The readers of the journal of John Wesley will remember that he, on several occasions, claimed to have seen the apparitions of his friends. The author has nothing to offer, but merely states the facts.]

EMILY'S FAREWELL.

I AM going across the river,
    Will you come, will you come!
Dear friends are waiting anxiously,
    Beck'ning home, beck'ning home.
Oh! see their arms outstretched for me,
    I'll away, I'll away;
Quick! trim the boat, the water's free,
    Don't delay, don't delay.

One has a chaplet in her hand,
    That's for me, that's for me,
When on the shore of that bright land,
    Ever free, ever free.
Oh! see that robe another holds!
    That is mine, that is mine;
Mark how the gems enrich the folds—
    Bright, divine; bright, divine.

Not long I've trod this earthly plane—
    Yet too long, yet too long,
I've had to bear its pangs and pain,
    Midst the throng, midst the throng.

Yet I've striven for the good,
  Fought the fight, fought the fight;
When foes stood by in threat'ning mood;
  Diffused the light, diffused the light.

Dear father, watch thy daughter's flight,
  Not in tears, not in tears;
For I shall dwell in endless light
  In the spheres, in the spheres.
Hark! hear that music on the air
  My requiem swell, my requiem swell:
O! think of me when I am there!
  Fare thee well, fare thee well.

Truth Ever Wins!

JOIN thy young life with those whose soul can ever prove
    a friend,
Evolve thy nature's own control, thine honor e'er defend.
A flatterer's tongue may lead astray, and wreck thy budding
    life.
Now watch thee those who would betray, or fill thy path
    with strife.

Make this a motto for thy home, and in thy chamber place;
Unite in peace whoe'er shall come: "Truth ever wins the race."
Respect thyself tho' friends may chide: do right and never
    fear;
Remember that the world is wide, though shadows may
    appear;
An honest heart on life's rough sea will ever win its way,
Youth's shadows may envelope thee, but hope thy life must
    sway.

[The winter of 1889 and 1890 was exceedingly mild, not only in Indiana but in the neighboring states. The following poems were written to commemorate that remarkable season.]

THE WAIL OF THE SEASON.

OH! where has the wanderer gone?
    For weeks I have wished his return.
I have basked in the meadows alone,
    While the winds of January burn.
Adown by the rippling stream,
    Soft zephyrs are fanning my head,
While a mantle of emerald green
    O'er mountain and valley is spread.
A bouquet of pansies I culled,
    With golden taraxicums twined,
And the bull-thistle's casket I hulled,
    And its thistle down blew to the wind.
The gossamers spread o'er the grass,
    Betipped with the dews of the morn,
And the mercury rose in the glass
    When the last of the decades was born.
I love thee, dear Winter, and yet
    I'm afraid thou art fickle and free,
For the Gulf-stream, a wicked coquette,
    Has oft set her bonnet for thee.
Oh, come back, my lover, to me!
    The sleigh and the robes I'll prepare,
And the waters o'er meadow and lea,
    The steel-footed skaters shall bear;
I will pile up the snow on the banks,
    And the school-boy shall slide on the pool,
And the farmer in spring shall give thanks
    That my darling old Winter did rule.
I'm afraid that thy cousin, young Spring,
    Is aiming to shorten thy reign;
Let the sleigh-bells merrily ring,
    And welcome my lover again!

WELCOME TO WINTER.

THE sleigh-bells are merrily ringing,
 My lover Old Winter hath come,
And the beautiful icicles clinging,
 To the eaves of every home.

I have waited so long thy returning,
 And anxiously watch'd every day,
My heart throbs, my bosom was burning,
 And wonder'd what caused thy delay.

But I woke from my couch in the morning,
 When January brought me her snow,
And the frost-king began his adorning,
 Of the panes of the rich and the low.

I knew that my friends were rejoicing,
 And sharing their gladness with me.
And the winds my wishes were voicing,
 The while I was waiting for thee.

Come lay thy white head on my breast,
 And tell me once more thou art mine.
I know thou wilt grant my request,
 And my love in return shall be thine.

The lakes and the rivers were waiting,
 To yield to thy wonted embrace.
And the school-boys who long'd for their skating,
 Now gleefully smile on thy face.

The trees in the woods and the glens,
 And the velvety grass on the plain
Awaited thy crystalline gems,
 To embellish their bodies again.

May thy coming be-gladden each soul,
 Of those who have watched thy return,
And joy lead them on to its goal,
 Where the bright fires of hope ever burn.

And the "little pigs to market,"
"Tweeking" made the young heart bound.

TO THE NEW YEAR, 1890.

WE watched last night thy elder brother's death ;
     The while the midnight bells entoned the air,
And vesper hymns borne on a nation's breath,
   Betold thy birth into this world of care.
Thou com'st to us a child of hidden fate,
   Our hopes and fears now on thy shoulders lay,
The hands of Time in silence we await,
   And henceforth all thy mandates must obey.
We laid thy brother on a flower decked bier,
   And wrapp'd his corpse in robes of vernal hue,
Nor glassy ice, nor flaky snows were there,
   But sunny spring clasped hands with him and you.
Winter delayed his journey round the world,
   And meadow-blossoms decked thy infant bed ;
While blighting care his sad'ning banner furled,
   And peace and joy their mirthful moments spread.
. Want stood aside and sorrow's tears were dried,
   And love and hope their robes about thee threw :
Thy brother's hand they grasped the while he died
   And held thine own, while into life you grew.

MOTHER'S TEACHINGS.

BY a bedside, in the gloaming,
     When the shadows of the night
Played around the window curtains,
   Clothing all in calm delight,
Sat a mother with her offspring,
   Listening to old nursery tales ;
Tales that every gray-haired parent
   Backward reads through memory's veils ;
When the lisping tongue was bridled,
   And the young ears caught the sound,
And the " Little Pigs to Market,"
   " Tweeking " made the young heart bound.

Then began the life-long lesson,
  To be good was to be loved ;
And that lesson well remembered,
  E'er a beacon light hath proved.
Mothers, ye who mould our being,
  From your laps the nations spring ;
'Tis to you we look for progress,
  Ye can peace or sorrow bring ;
Yours the sceptre, yours the crown,
  Yours the hand and heart to guide,
By your precepts, by your lives,
  Spread the temperance doctrine wide.

BEAUTY.

I KNOW not why, Philosophers declare
  That Beauty is but skin deep to the view ;
Nor why they paint a vision of despair,
  When time shall scar the cheek of tinted hue.

The snowy brow, the graceful swanlike neck,
  And glossy curls, that o'er the shoulders wave,
Are but the gems with which our God did deck
  That noble gift which he to Adam gave.

'Tis in the deep recesses of the soul,
  Where we alone unsullied beauty trace,
Where streams of love unfeigned forever roll,
  Though grey the locks and furrowed be the face.

True beauty rare we find in woman's love,
  When hard our fate midst sickness and distress,
Then her sweet voice like music from above,
  Can soothe our cares and every moment bless.

Then say no more that beauty e'er can fade,
  For beauty lies deep hidden from your gaze ;
But give your love unfetter'd to the maid,
  And beauty's charms will claim your endless praise.

" The sombre curtains of the night moved zephyr-like without a pause,
Then 'neath an arch of crimson light Sunbeam appeared with Santa Claus.''

Birth and Adventures of Santa Claus.

FAR, far away in distant ages, before the life of man was
known,
With none to paint the picture-pages for which our children
now are prone,
Time, out in space, all sad and lonely, moved slowly through
the universe ;
Conscious ever that he only with God and angels could
converse.
Being weary of a single life, the palace of the Sun he sought,
Determined to find therein a wife, and with him his creden-
tials brought.
Old Sol, with beaming, bright expression — the gray-beard
saw and welcomed him,
And quick prepared a grand procession of laughing, chubby
cherubim.
Now Sunbeam was the oldest daughter, who marshal'd on
the glittering throng ;
With harps the Seraphim besought her and cheer'd the angel
band with song.
A glittering conclave graced the throne when Sol the happy
swain addressed—
"Time : My daughter, Sunbeam, is thine own ; with deathless life be each possessed."

Here in my celestial home has earth's first nuptial knot been
tied,
From out my courts shall worlds unknown, the deathless
universe divide ;
Each world shall be to each a light ; thou, Time, by marriage made my son,
Shall mark the nations in their flight, while worlds shall
crumble, one by one.
The queen of seraphs and thy bride with thee shall back to
earth repair,
And magic wands I will provide that shall protect them everywhere.

The source of life they shall control, and beings rise at their
    command,
And joy shall fill each life-wrought soul and shower its bless-
    ings o'er the land.
The seraph queen, a fairy now, shall wingless on the earth
    reside,
And she my mandates will avow and e'er protect thee and
    thy bride ;
The soil thy every want shall yield and all thy human hosts
    maintain,
And endless life shall be revealed to every soul on earth's
    domain.

Tho' older than his father-in-law, old Time was ever blithe
    and gay,
And in the crystal ice he saw his hair and beard were snowy
    gray.
Now Sunbeam and Time a counsel held in a broad cave of
    clefted ice ;
By fairies and fays they were bespel'd, but fought against
    each elf's device.
They each wished a son that should embrace sleek, snowy
    locks and sunlit face,
Wherein old age and youth may trace enwisdom'd years and
    youthful grace.
Now Sunbeam back to her father hied and met him as he left
    his throne ;
Old Sol, through the aisle his daughter 'spied, whose radiant
    face majestic shone ;
He read her wish in every line like words congealed upon
    her brow—
"Thy heart's desire is already thine ; husband and son await
    thee now ;
Hie thee a-back to the Northland wild ; thy love hath won
    thy noble cause,
And honor thy earth-bound, mystic child with the deathless
    name of Santa Claus."

Now Sunbeam grasp'd her wings of light and pin'd them to
    her fairy form ;
Her pinions gleamed with radiance bright while earthward
    riding on the storm.

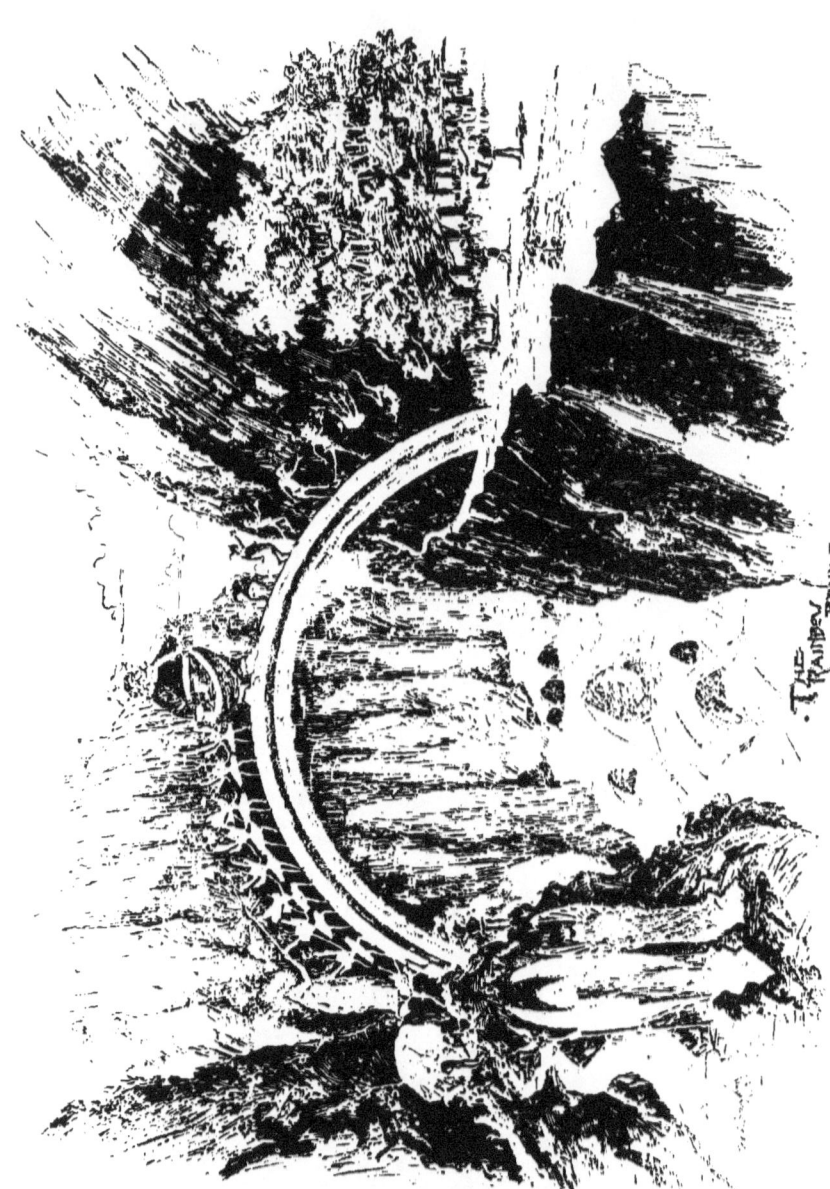

THE RAINBOW BRIDGE.

"Sunbeam her magic wand display'd, and waved it o'er the deep ravine,
With gorgeous bands of light arrayed, a rainbow bridge at once was seen."

Time waited now with yearning heart the safe returning of
    his bride,
When he beheld, with sudden start, Aurora's flood gates
    open wide :
The sombre curtains of the night moved zephyr-like without
    a pause,
Then 'neath an arch of crimson light Sunbeam appeared with
    Santa Claus.
From icy gorge and crystal cave sweet fairy music fill'd the
    air,
And Time a rapturous welcome gave and clasped with joy
    his new-found heir.
From rocks and hills on every side mischievous elfs and fays
    were seen,
Yet Santa Claus in their gambols vied and wish'd that he a
    child had been.
Old Time replied in language mild when Santa Claus himself
    expressed :
"Thou art my son, both man and child ; through thee shall
    unborn babes be bless'd."

Across a chasm broad and deep, a pine-tree forest rear'd its
    head
And foaming waters down the steep with thundering rush
    the torrent sped.
Now Santa Claus beheld the land luxuriant with moss and
    fern,
While Sunbeam called her elfin band and would from each
    their wishes learn :
With one accord they all declared that they would through
    the forest roam,
The thought of crossing, each one scared as they look'd be-
    low on the boiling foam.
Sunbeam her magic wand display'd and waved it o'er the
    deep ravine ;
With gorgeous bands of light arrayed a rainbow bridge at
    once was seen ;
A shout of joy now fill'd the air and echo backward threw
    the sound,
Ten thousand tiny feet were there who sought the bridge
    with magic bound.

Now every one of all the band had safely cross'd the deep
    abyss;
For greenwoods wild and forest land they left the ice-bound
    wilderness.

Like pilgrims from a distant land safe settled on a friendly
    shore,
They call'd together all the band and plan'd the country to
    explore.
The fairies hushed their tinkling bells and all the little elfs
    obeyed;
Deep silence reigned o'er hills and dells while they their new-
    found home survey'd.
"This is a land of rare delights," said Sunbeam, as she
    glanced around;
"Such stream-cleft vales and mossy heights can nowhere on
    the earth be found;
But are we sure that we can gain a title to this Paradise?
Others no doubt have laid their claim—we cannot be the
    only wise."
Time listened to his wife's address, and very sagely thus re-
    plied:
"This is the land of happiness; its rights to none can be de-
    nied;
The good of every land may come and claim a right on its
    domain,
But guilt can never find a home; the pure alone can entrance
    gain."

Pale Twilight, daughter of the Moon, riding on the zephyrs
    came,
And sleepy Night approaching soon bid every glow-worm
    raise his flame;
Tired Nature now soon sank in rest, while Vigils hung their
    lamps in space—
The night owls then began their quest among the new incom-
    ing race.
Aurora, harbinger of day, aroused the band with music rare;
The song birds tuned their morning lay and joy was present
    everywhere.
They bathed them in the morning dews, from silvery streams
    their thirst allay'd,
And Nectar, from the trees profuse, a banquet rare for each
    one made.

"Yet Santa Claus in their gambols vied, and wished that he a child had been."

Such was the home of Santa Claus, from whence the friend
    of childhood came;
'Twas here he framed his changeless laws and here began his
    deathless fame;
His workshops here in sylvan dells surrounded by an elfin
    band;
Here friendly fairies worked their spells and spread their
    joys throughout the land.

The clefted rocks on the mountain side had left a league of
    mossy land
Through which the silvery streamlets glide, with trees and
    shrubs on every hand;
Now Santa Claus the land survey'd, before his parents laid
    his plan,
And elfs and fays his word obey'd, and now his life-long
    work began;
Nor axe nor plane, nor saw nor spade, nor tool of any kind
    had they.
He therefore sought the fairies' aid, and his request before
    them lay.
The fairy queen her promise gave that all his needs would be
    supplied;
"We'll bear thee to the giant's cave—naught that thou wish
    shall be denied."
They led him through a cavern deep, where glow-worm
    lamps were spread around,
And there the giant fast asleep was quickly by the fairies
    bound;
His axe and spear were at his feet, and all his tools about
    him lay,
With these they made a safe retreat and sought once more
    the open day.

They hied them to their chosen glade and there a solem coun-
    cil held,
And all their future plans were laid, and marked the trees
    that should be fell'd.
Up through the vale with ponderous tread they quick beheld
    the giant's form,
The elfs and fays in terror sped, but naught could Santa
    Claus alarm;

He on the fairy queen relied, who promised ever to defend,
And when the giant he espied, he called upon his fairy friend.
As quick as thought the fairy came and smote the giant as he
　　stood ;
He fell beneath her faultless aim, and rising sought the dis-
　　tant wood.
"Stay, tyrant, stay," the fairy cried; "look in the stream —
　　thy horns survey !
A reindeer now on the mountain side, our Santa Claus thou
　　shalt obey."
They plucked the fronds of maiden hair and wove a girth
　　and bridle strong,
And led him to a new-made lair form'd by the elfins' busy
　　throng.

Their labors now they could pursue, quite heedless of the
　　giant's will—
A happier band none ever knew, nor purer hearts could
　　pleasure thrill.
So deftly every hand was plied in weaving moss with maiden
　　hair ;
From this their garments were supplied and all their hang-
　　ings rich and rare,
With ivy strands from tree to tree and trailing woodbines
　　trellised o'er.
A prettier home you could not see—no human heart could
　　wish for more.
Nor wonder now that Santa Claus should with his labor be
　　inspired ;
With elfs and fairies in his cause he'd make what every
　　child desired ;
He cleft his wood in every form, and toys beneath his fingers
　　grew,
And colors every eye to charm from wings of butterflies he
　　drew.
The fairies always paint the toys, the elfs the whips and
　　whistles make—
The elfs, you know, are fairy boys, that's why they this
　　position take.

" Stay, tyrant, stay ! " the fairy cried : " look in the stream, thy horns survey !
A reindeer now on the mountain side, our Santa Claus thou shalt obey."

"Then started off without a pause, and o'er the mountains bent his way."

Now, when the toys were all prepared, close packed in pack-
     ages they lay,
And all who in the labors shared began to look for Christ-
     mas-day.
Then Santa Claus began to build a sleigh of mountain ash
     and oak,
And every heart with wonder fill'd as fell his axe with
     measured stroke.
Fairies nor elfs could give their aid in labor such as now was
     needed,
So a visit to the reindeer paid, anxious to know how he suc-
     ceeded.

He toss'd his head in haughty pride as though he knew his
     wond'rous change,
And had he not been safely tied he would across the moun-
     tains range.
Now Santa Claus, his sleigh completed, with all the trap-
     pings tight and trim,
And fays and fairies soon were seated, determined they
     would ride with him.
The reindeer pranced while Santa Claus affixed the traces to
     the sleigh,
Then started off without a pause, and o'er the mountains
     bent his way.

O'er hills and vales, with lightning speed, the reindeer drew
     his load with ease,
And all the elfin band agreed that they the fairy queen would
     please.
And now they turned, their home to reach, all gladdened
     with their first attempt ;
Determined now the world to teach that youth should be
     from cares exempt ;
And Santa Claus agreed to do whate'er the faries should pro-
     claim ;
Then they a solemn contract drew and Santa Claus affix'd
     his name :

"I, Santa Claus, do here declare that I will make all sorts
　　　　of toys
And spread them broadcast everywhere at Christmas-tide
　　　　among the boys;
The girls shall have their skipping ropes, their cradles and
　　　　all sorts of dolls,
And bows and ties and scented soaps and croquet sets and
　　　　tennis balls;
With reindeer speed at night I'll come and drop my presents
　　　　down the flue,
Then hie me back to my Northland home, and every year
　　　　my ride renew."

Now Christmas-tide being near at hand, the fairy queen his
　　　　workshop sought,
Where Santa Claus and his elfin band the labors of the year
　　　　had brought,
"I sought thee here," the fairy cried, "to place this charm
　　　　upon thy breast,
That when thou goest upon thy ride, thy every moment shall
　　　　be blest;
Fear not the rugged cliff nor vale, but press thee on with
　　　　lightning speed;
Against this charm naught can prevail, and joy shall crown
　　　　thy every deed."

And now they formed a fairy ring while Santa Claus pre-
　　　　pared his sleigh;
Anxious, his airy flight to wing, the reindeer stood in trap-
　　　　pings gay;
The sleigh bells breathed their silvery notes and echo caught
　　　　the magic sound;
An elfin shout from a thousand throats, rang through the
　　　　hills and vales around;
But naught could stay his onward flight, for Christmas eve
　　　　was close at hand,
And all his presents, on that night, must be delivered
　　　　through the land.

" The rosy faced boy, sent early to school,
His satchel lays down to slide on the pool,
Quite heedless of tasks to be done."

WINTER.

[Written in London, 1862, during a severe winter, when thousands were starving.]

BOREAS now rides on the gray, cold clouds;
  Pale Phœbus is wrapt in the twining shrouds
    Of Winter's relentless weaving.
To the frescoed porch and the ivied eaves,
To the evergreen shrubs and their burden'd leaves,
    The glistening icicle's cleaving.

The trees seem to mourn their vestures of white,
And robin in vain seeks a place to alight—
    The earth-worm to pluck for a meal.
The velvet piled green now cracks 'neath our feet;
The swamp covered meadows the skaters now greet—
    One pleasure of winter to feel.

The rosy faced boy, sent early to school,
His satchel lays down to slide on the pool,
    Quite heedless of tasks to be done;
The fast falling snow now fills him with glee,
Tho' swollen his hands, light hearted and free,
    He joins in the snow-balling fun.

My lady looks out from her damask'd cloth'd panes,
My lord with his gun scours mountains and plains,
    For winter brings pleasure to them;
'Tis theirs not to feel the season's rough course—
The tempest may roar, but spent is its force
    On the labor bound portion of men.

Our shops may be stored for the feasts of the few,
But Christmas his sorrows will ever bestrew,
    While revelry seems to abound.
Our rivers are block'd and clos'd are our wharves,
The laborer begs or his family starves,
    As surely as winter comes round.

The pale faced mechanic now grieves for his boy,
Who clamours for bread through the lack of employ,
   Which vainly he seeks to obtain;
His daughter and wife, with needle and thread,
O'er mantle or shirt now plies for their bread,
   A pauperized pittance to gain.

MOUNT CONGREVE.

AN ACROSTIC.

M USE of Ossian, lend thine aid!
    Wander with me through the glade,
O'er these woods and streams preside,
   Call the naiads to my side.
Up from out these fairy dells,
   Bid the wood-nymphs weave their spells.
Now let fair Echo rule the glen,
   And Orpheus tune his pipes again,
That every hill and every tree
   Resound the fairy minstrelsy.
Come around the beech-tree hill,
   Where blooms the modest daffodil.
O'er my lyre thy fingers trace,
   And sing its beauties and its grace;
Nature here her banquet spread,
   When the gods from heaven were led.
Groves of nectar-dripping trees
   Supplied their feasting revelries;
Round the river's margin'd side,
   Where the Suir's sweet waters glide,
Each evening sun unveils her breast,
   And sinks on Congreve's lap to rest.
Vesper notes from rustling leaves
   Are borne upon each passing breeze;
E'en night forgets his gloom to spread
   O'er Congreve's still, sequestered bed.

THE ELFIN GLADE.

A REVERIE.

[Written at Excelsior Springs, Mo.]

I 'LL hie me to the Elfin glade,
 Where flows the Fishing River,
And there beneath the elm trees' shade
 The cares of life will sever.

The toil and din of city life,
 I'll banish for a season,
And once forget the wiles and strife
 That warp the trader's reason.

The stories of my childhood days
 Around my brain will hover,
While Ariel sprites through fancy's maze
 Will backward bring my lover.

With joy I'll pace the sylvan dell,
 Where the snake-like rootlets climb,
And o'er again my love tales tell,
 As back in my youth's young prime.

The fairy rings by rootlets formed,
 Will chain my mind forever,
And e'en forget how fortune stormed
 When she our loves did sever.

'Twas 'neath such stately elms as these
 My love's first hopes were spoken,
And backward now my memory flees,
 E'en tho' her vows were broken.

With rope-like stems and trellis'd strands
 With weird fantastic twinings,
Beseems the work of fairy hands,
 And elfin king's designings.

Oh, that the human heart was true
  As are the elm branch twinings,
The love of years would e'er be new,
  Bereft of sorrow's pinings.

Though time hath clothed my wrinkled brow
  With whitened locks dishevel'd,
I fain would seek that valley now,
  Where in my youth I revel'd.

That cannot be—but I will seek
  Missouri's wond'rous stream,
Where one and all alike bespeak
  The home of our life's young dream.

The ancient sire and aged dame,
  Or earth's fair sons and daughters,
May life prolong and health reclaim
  Through Regent's magic waters.

From out a shady winding dell
  These wond'rous springs are welling,
No pen can write nor tongue can tell
  How hearts with joy are swelling.

Disease in all its varied forms,
  Presaging death and sorrow,
Must yield to Regent Water's charms,
  And joy and peace will follow.

THE AGNOSTIC.

AN ACROSTIC ON THOUGHT.

[This was written after a debate on the subject of the sin against the Holy Ghost between the author and a Roman Catholic student named Henry John Edward Salmon, then living at Cowes, on the Isle of Wight.]

HOW vast the sphere of human thought.
    A boundless region undefined,
Enveloped and with wonder fraught,
    Are all the workings of the mind.
Nor can we tell from whence they spring ;
    That they exist is all we know.
Ransomless our thoughts will cling,
    Tho' rapid as the winds they flow,
Yet while we watch the seasons roll
    Each year discloses to our gaze,
Journeying onward to its goal,
    Some noble mind that claimed our praise.
Oh, could I soar that vaulted dome,
    Wherein they tell me spirits dwell,
How gladly would I seek that home ;
    But 'gainst such things my thoughts rebel.
Ne'er say again that guilty I
    Before a throne must some day stand
Expectant in some hell to lie
    For thoughts o'er which I'd no command.
Did my rude thoughts to me disclose
    The dwelling of a spirit God
Where natureless I could repose
    Beyond the limits of the sod?
All my actions pure and holy
    Ever in His sight should be,
Restless till I'd reach that glory,
    There from cares and sorrow free.
Doom'd by fate the thought to cherish
    That there is naught beyond the grave,
Shall my poor form in torment perish,
    Or in a fiery ocean lave.

Ah, be there God, my heart can tell,
  I can nor shape nor figure give.
Lo, would I seek, but thoughts rebel,
  Nor spirit with my mind can live :
My mind can never soar beyond
  The limits of this earthly sphere.
On Nature's works I'd raise a song,
  For they to me are ever dear,
Nor will I fail while traveling on
  To shun the bad and good revere.

CARES ARE WEEDS.

CARES are weeds in nature's garden,
  Mingling with the fruits of life ;
Laid in ambush for the conflict.
  Soldiers, born of human strife.
All the joys of earth and heaven,
  Catch the shadows of their cares :
Rest is found not in the gloaming,
  Till the corn uproots the tares ;
And the midday sun of progress,
  Rise above us unawares.

All the teachings of the ages,
  Prove the spirit life of mortals ;
Never dying, ever changing
  Through our life's e'er changing portals ;
Now the earth-life with its anguish,
  Crush the good from out the soul :
Envy, spleen and passion's breathings
  Bid us seek our spirit's goal.

MY CHILDHOOD'S HOME.

COULD I back to the home of my childhood repair,
   And again hear the music that floats on the air ;
Hear the sound of the billows that roll o'er the beach,
   Lock'd in by the mountain, far as vision can reach ;
Again from the valley climb up o'er the hill,
   Inspired by the thoughts which my memories thrill ;
Repeat in my fancies, all the joys of my youth ;
   Call back all the heart-throbs ever deathless as truth ;
Let Nelson's high column looking out o'er the sea
   Enwrap me with pleasures long banished from me ;
Even though my possessions may shield me from care,
Sunny Hampshire to thee I would gladly repair.

Remote though the time when my cousins and I
   Roamed out o'er the strand while the vessels sailed by ;
I see in my fancy the fishermen still,
   Inspecting their nets at the foot of the hill.
Valley, mountain and meadow, bestrewn with their flowers,
   Veiled the shadows of life from youth's happy hours ;
E'en though when I left for my now foster home
   Earth sought my loved cousin and claimed him her own,
Remembrance aback to my childhood returns,
   Roda's sweet breath from her kisses still burns
Sweet as the dewdrops which the meadows bestrew,
   Soft kissing the flowers in spring time anew.

Bear me back in my dreams o'er the billowy deep,
   Breathe the voices of friends midst the silence of sleep;
Recall the broad landscape o'er which I would roam,
   Repeat all the joys of my youth's early home.
Out over the waters the sweet isle of Wight,
   On the bosom of ocean looms up to the sight ;
Old Thistlewaite's Halls through England renowned ;
   On Portsmouth and Southsea my visions seem bound.
Kindly dear Nature to thee I appeal,
   Keep constant the visions my childhood reveal ;
Earth and its bounties are nothing to me,
   Effaced from the thoughts of my home o'er the sea.

5 -

AN ACROSTIC TO WILLIAM GARDINER.

[A good man, a constant friend, but with unfortunate habits, who
several years after the following was written committed suicide on Yar-
mouth Sands.]

WHENE'ER a man can boast his gold,
   He no lack of friends will find;
If on life's stage dull scenes unfold,
   Gold will waft them to the wind.
Let liberty—old England's pride—
   Further spread her sacred boon;
Let men of wealth no longer chide
   The man who share's misfortune's doom.
Insatiate wealth, howe'er attained,
   Will find the vilest villain friends;
And honest poverty 's disdained,
   While want into a crime extends.
Misfortune—curse of all mankind—
   Seldom comes if left unsought;
Grief, poverty and woe, combined,
   Oft by men are dearly bought.
And many have that secret found,
   But to know it was too late;
Reflection's voice, with maddening sound,
   Comes but to tell the wretch his fate.
Desist from now the future ills
   That perchance your path may crop;
Imbibe no more the vice that fills
   The minds of men with loathsome dross.
Nor word nor action can be found
   To find us friends if fortune fail;
Eternal griefs and woes resound,
   And yet no friends your lot bewail.
Remember, while with fortune crown'd,
   The moral of my simple tale.

ETERNITY.

ETERNITY be thou my theme,
  Sole 'biding occupant of boundless space,
Dar'd I to contemplate thy mien
  What vivid fancies would my pencil trace ;
When thou were not, I dare not think,
  But that thou art, is graven on my soul,
And oft on reason's very brink
  Alluring fancies do my sense control.
Receding worlds now crowd my view,
  A pageant grand yet solemn to behold ;
Deep contemplations range anew,
  O'er buried landscapes ; science doth unfold
High mountain tops, and gorges deep ;
  What power could lift, or lower thee to thy place ;
Oh, thou blue vault where vigils keep
  Their glittering watch throughout ethereal space,
Lo, o'er thy vast empyrean sweep
  The footsteps of eternity we trace.
Look on the sod, see how it yields
  To man and beast what they in nature crave ;
And yet this drapery of the fields
  May be the atoms of some human grave.
Now on the rugged cloud-capp'd peaks,
  Where carrion vultures find a safe retreat,
Down in the ocean depths there sleeps
  Nations whose thoughts were but what we repeat.
Time, sister of eternity,
  When thou thy mighty, matchless power unsheath,
Heaps from the vale this mountain high,
  And at thy nod whole nations sink in death.
Oh, that proud men should seek to hide
  Their weakness 'neath some philosophic lie ;
Replete with seeming wisdom, chide
  Those who dare doubt their vague philosophy.

No single atom of this world
  Can lose its being in the universe
Howe'er from place to place 'tis hurl'd ;
  Its laws are fixed and certain in their course.
In the small stream, slow rippling by,
  In embryo we a mighty river see ;
Lash'd by the waves now surging high,
  Some rock long crumbled into sands descry :
Lo, here we catch one glimpse of thee,
  Thou strange, mysterious, dark eternity.

HOPE AGAINST FATE.

THE clock ticks on; the wheels of time
  Wait not the sluggard's pace,
For while they mourn their chances gone,
  The swift hath won the race.
Why sit ye down and mourn your fate,
  The world is long and wide,
And tho' each chance hath fail'd ye,
  Yet, another may be tried.
A pebble in the streamlet's course;
  An opening in the sand,
May guide the gushing rivulet
  Across the desert land;
Then there is wealth for all who try,
  No matter what their sphere;
With health and strength and God to guide,
  The weakest need not fear;
The selfsame sun that lights the King,
  Gives light to you and me.
The ambient air, the rustling breeze,
  Alike to all are free.
Then gird ye on with heart and hand,
  With work there's wealth in store;
While cringing Fate slow lags behind,
  Bright Hope runs on before.

ODE TO AMERICAN FLOUR.

See Genesis
Chap. xviii, 5-6
verses.

THE evening sun the plains of Mamre spread,
When unto Abraham three angels came.
"Sarah," he cried, "go fetch the strangers bread,"
She brought the meal and quickly baked the
same.

See the
last war in
Macedon.

But then the meal was coarse and rough and
strong,
The art of baking had not yet begun.
To Roman zeal these rising arts belong
When bakers' guilds throughout the empire sprung.

See Genesis
xl, verse 3.

When Pharaoh's baker in his prison lay
With Joseph bound by his relentless king,
Did then his clear Egyptian modes display.
From whence the art of baking thus did spring.

See the war
'gainst Perseus
Macedon.

But when the Roman chiefs from Macedon
Brought back to Rome the secrets of the trade,
The modern art of baking was begun
And bread from flour of Macedon was made.

See Pliny on
Vesuvius.

When Pompeii fell with lava beds o'erspread;
And flour and ovens in the scoria lay,
Through centuries past, we still can see the bread
As sweet and fresh as on that fatal day.

America
beats the
world in flour.

The Macedonian secret we've divined,
And brought to light the methods of the past,
With chosen cereals now of every kind,
We make a flour the world has ne'er surpassed.

[Note:—The following poem was written at Kansas City, Missouri, in commemoration of the festival of Pallas Athena, which is given annually during the month of October.]

An Ode.

TO PALLAS ATHENA, GODDESS OF ART AND INDUSTRY.

WELCOME, Athena, to our city of the hills,
     Be thou defender of our citadels;
Light as of yore the regions of the skies,
Expand thy arts through new industries.
Light up the minds of our advancing race
And bid Columbia from our city trace
A band of men whose thoughts shall rule the world;
These men, thy Priests, their banners have unfurled.
Thine was the light e'er Sun or Moon or Star
Lit up the blazoning ether near and far.
The universe was thine in which to play,
Child of the Light and Goddess of the Day.
As did the Romans visit at thy shrine,
The honored pilgrims both of thee and thine.
So shall our pilgrimage be bent to thee,
Athena, Pallas, Goddess of the Free.
Thy mother, Metis, swallowed by thy sire,
Burst from his brain in intellectual fire,
And thou, the child of Zeus, thus began
To educate the shadowed brains of man.
Hephæstion, Vulcan of the Ancient Greek,
The skull of Zeus, split from cheek to cheek.
Amidst the gods, on high Olympus then
Pallas Athena bore the stamp of men;
'Twas by thy touch the barren rocks did bear—
To Attica their olives, rich and rare
Food for the gods, and light for gloomy night
Won to thyself the evidence of might.
Thy temple still upon the crags of Greece
To man discloses all the arts of peace,
And we to-day, the Athens of the West,
Do give thee welcome, and at thy behest

Have built a shrine on our acropolis,
A beacon guide and harbinger of bliss.
When from thy shrine our sages shall advance
With wisdom, caught from thy embracing glance,
Then from our vales the factory walls will rise
And school and college prove our enterprise.
But first to gain the value of thy light
Are those whose orbs are weakening of their sight,
To them thy bright Actinic rays will prove
The deathless evidence of lasting love;
As on thy shield the slain Medusa's head
Tells of thy conquest of the falling dead,
So shall thy light unto the race unborn
Prove to thoughtless men a constant thorn.

*   *   *   *   *   *   *

But now we fain would ask why Neptune comes with
    thee;
Hast thou the circus of Flaminis been to see?
Or hast thou tarried in the temple standing by
Where Neptunalia is rehearsed through each July?
If so, indeed, we're sorry for thy lack of sense
To take a bastard Roman god as recompense.
Thine Uncle Posiedon with Nereus should have come
With all his fifty smiling daughters to our home;
Their leaping dolphin steeds with manes of shining
    gold,
Whose opal diadems each Naiad brow enfold;
Then would the aim of our Missourian merchants be
More truly pictured in thy Western revelry.
Perhaps our seeming harsh critiques are in advance
And that thou aimst our lagging city to advance.
Thou might'st have meant our common council to re-
    place
And show the monstrous boodling, board of works
    disgrace.
Or seeking Hoover's tank of thrice-paid gasoline
To show how half-dressed stones on our new courts
    are seen.

We know that honest men have vetoed many schemes
And many itching palms have closed like morning
   dreams.
Hadst thou thy kinsman brought, the "noble Hercules,"
Our Augean stables, then, their stench would soon
   release,
And many constables fresh from felon's cell
Would fall before the courts their blackmail tales to
   tell ;
Nor drunken justice more would our fair courts dis-
   grace
By selling at the bar his whiskers off his face.*
No doubt thou'st heard of spreading grip-slots in our
   streets
And man-traps on our avenues where death repeats
The solemn, silent story of a neighbor dead,
Through unfilled roadside ditch or cable-slot out-spread.
This is the glorious privilege of being free —
Free to accept what boodle aldermen decree.
And yet we feel the adage of the world gone by —
'Twere better not by far o'er wasted milk to cry ;
What is, is done, and we our wants and hopes have
   told
With honest tongue and language free, tho' seeming
   bold.
Then backward to the crags of Greece with lightning
   speed,
And tell thy father, Zeus, of our nation's need,
While we in turn will aid his constant sore distress,
And o'er Olympian heights spread constant happiness.
Take back the promised prize thou com'st so far to
   gain,
Wherewith thy honored sire may banish all his pain.
Our famed city, then, with all its glories spread,
And Greece once more revive the memories of its dead.
Farewell once more, loved Goddess of Land and Sea,
And when next year thou comest we'll greet thee
   merrily.

---

*It is a fact that a drunken justice did sell for whiskey the whiskers off
his face. This was at the time a joke in every bar-room in the neighborhood.

THE PROMISES OF SPRING.

MAY-FLOWERS shall bloom amid the thorns, and all
their fragrance shed;
  Field daisies, harbingers of Spring, our vernal fields o'er-
    spread ;
And song birds tune their morning lays to form Aurora's
  choir ;
  Entrancing music of the spheres, their varied notes inspire.
Replete with joy from Winter's gloom, we'll meet the glad-
  some Spring,
  Laughing at care and sorrows past, a life of hope begin ;
Young hearts shall leap like sun-warmed buds, beneath ceru
  lean skies ;
  Impassioned love on angel wings, shall speed their des-
    tinies.
  Cold Winter's blast and gloomy Night must soon their
    cycles run ;
  Invidious Care shall hide his head from Laughter's romping
    son,
  And maiden Spring, midst blossoms rare, a "charming
    girl," will come.
The sun-tipped waters of the vales, brushed by the perfumed
  breeze,
  Shall lure us to their moss-grown banks, midst pensive
    reveries.
Hands locked in hands, with sunlit hearts, soul-'rapped within
  the dales,
  Heaven's foretaste of happiness, be told in lovers' tales.
Olympian heights, where gods of yore attuned their harps
  in song,
  And fields Elysian—no more to mortal men belong,
Revolving worlds must e'er maintain their journey 'mong the
  spheres ;
  Wisdom and love in sweet refrain, attune our passing
    years.
New hopes and joys shall e'er arise, while truth our hearts
  control ;
  Eternal peace beyond the skies, awaits the truthful soul.

MOTHER AND DAUGHTER.

SEEKING A REUNION.

HEARKEN to the angel music ; list to its seraphic tones ;
   All the world is watching o'er our labors and our homes ;
Not a thought or word is uttered but is registered forever ;
Not a deed of guilt or kindness can we from our record sever ;
As we fill our earthly mission, so our future home will be ;
Heaven is every soul's belonging—we build our own eternity.

Why should men be e'er repining, why not grasp the earth's
      delights ;
Earth is paradise to all men who would give to each his rights ;
Eternal joy is nature's birthright, with the music of the
      spheres ;
Kindness are the angel vestments that beclothe our fleeting
      years ;
Sin too often ope's the fountain of our sorrows and our tears.

Every flower that decks the meadows, every tree on mountain
      side,
Lends its aid our lives to brighten, each a beacon and a guide ;
Lost are they who ever mourning for the loved ones gone
      before,
And forgetting how unbounding are the memories in store.

When from earth we join our loved ones, there to meet and
      part no more,
Eternal hope should fill the breast, undying truth should
      mould the soul ;
Earth's bounteous fruits are spread for all and heaven the
      haven and the goal ;
Keep then thy heart on loved ones gone, and work a better
      world to leave ;
Seek thou a sceptre and a crown and a spotless garment
      weave.

MORAL MUSINGS.

HOPE for the better and work to the end,
  Make every effort mankind to defend ;
All that's within us our actions should show
  A spirit of love mongst those that we know.
Render to others the rights you demand,
  Unite and be men, true hearts to command.
Vice overcometh when selfishness reigns ;
  Right rules triumphant o'er nature's domains ;
Empires and Nations may rule for the day,
  Enrapturing success may lead us astray,
Yet the near future beglimmers a light,
  Thinning the shadows, dissolving the night,
  And justice and law must rule for the right.

Envy and malice may rancor within ;
  Lust and its evils may clothe us in sin ;
Ubiquitous self may enter each soul,
  And charity cease the heart to control.
God may be doubted his love to bestow ;
  Umbrage 'mongst mortals may constantly grow ;
E'en kindred and friends their creeds may divide,
  Brother his brother may each one deride.
No joy for this world, no hope in the spheres,
  An indwelling doubt may grow with our years.
Empyrean light may never disclose
  Conceptions of God, in whom we repose—
  Heaven will e'er be a myth unto those.

But few are the minds who look upon earth,
  Boundless in beauty and priceless in worth,
Attempt to deny the fiat of God,
  Asserting His will through motionless sod.
Revolving in space, in orbits unknown,
  Rending the heavens, are worlds like our own.

The atoms of suns the universe fill,
   Thus the creation can never stand still.
Hearts may be mingled in hope and in love,
   Hearts may be severed on earth or above ;
Only a sentence in anger expressed,
   Or one thoughtless word to loved ones address'd,
Life-times of sorrow in many a home,
   Left its cold impress when loved ones would roam.
Our words spoke in jest may shatter the life
   Of husband, or friend, or sister, or wife.
May God in his might mould every soul,
   May men among men their passions control.
Enjoin every heart that man never dies,
   Evolved from the earth to dwell in the skies,
Where lov'd ones shall meet in realms of the blest,
   When death calls us hence with spirits to rest.

CORRECT ORTHOEPY.

EDWARD B. WARMAN, B. A.

DOUBLE ACROSTIC.

COUNT not the power of language or thought,
 Expressed in an unpolished tone.
Our measures of force, by methods are wrought,
 Drawn not from the subject alone.
Respect for the sense of the thought in review,
 Will cause you its force to maintain;
Refinement will then every study bestrew,
 And speech all its beauty attain.
Engrave on your mind the factors of sound;
 Refer every word to the ear;
Cull figures of speech neither coarse nor profound;
 Do not as a pedant appear.
Then will the power of each sentence be felt,
 By all whom your language shall hear.

Out from the atoms evolved from the brain,
 We mould every sound we desire;
Responsive to will, every effort's a gain,
 And Orthoepy all can acquire.
That thought is creative all nature proclaims,
 Reviled though the statement may be;
Held in the realm of the magnet's domains,
 Mind, matter and thought we can see.
Our organs of sense in number have grown,
 And the magnet—the sense of the soul—
Evolves through the mind that thought may be shown,
 Nearing life to its ultimate goal.
Preserve in your thought the right rulings of speech,
 And mould every sense to its law.
Your aim e'er should be a perfection to reach,
 Making sure of your hearers' eclat.

[This was written at the request of E. B. Warman, the author of "War-man's Correct Orthoepy."]

To Edgar Allen Poe.

DOUBLE ACROSTIC.

E'EN as the Greeks a fabled Homer claimed,
   Erin hath e'er her mystic Ossian famed ;
Depicting each, in mythologic phrase,
   Disastrous strife or measured roundelays,
God-given poesy of love and worth
   Waited the Soul of Poe to give it birth ;
And he, the child of care, his mission filled,
   And nations' hearts his magic numbers thrilled.
Remorseless critics, jealous of his fame,
   Rumored their lies and smirched his deathless name.
An adverse fortune lent its cruel aid,
   Deepening the charge upon his shoulders laid.
Let venomed hearts pour out their vials of gall,
   Bid coward tongues the rights of truth enthrall.
Let lying scribblers blot his deathless page,
   While yet his foes a shameless battle wage,
Æolian harps, from angel hands, will sound
   An anthem through the world's remotest bound.
Nations unborn their pæons will rehearse,
   Replete in praise of Poe's unequaled verse,
Pour out their souls in heav'n dictated song,
   Make mountains echo all the vales along ;
Olympian music, from the distant spheres,
   Attune his poems through recurring years.
E'en though maligned by Griswold's false memoir,
   New friends will stay his foes' relentless war.

Chicago, July 4th, 1889.

[The above poem was suggested to the author on reading the advance
sheets of Prof. Warman's book (then in press) entitled "Critical Analysis of
Poe's 'Raven,' and Memoir of Poe."]

"THE WOODMAN'S WELCOME."

DOUBLE ACROSTIC.

TAKE thee a seat, my Neighbor and my friend.
　　Join our repast, tho' humble it may be;
Here our Camp-fire its genial warmth will lend;
　　Our hearts with thine shall beat in unity.
Earth yields its fruits to labor's honest toil;
　　Sweet is the sleep which conscious duties bring;
Man's life depends upon the well till'd soil,
　　E'en tho' our cities magic-like may spring,
Our own strong arms the Axe and Beetle wield,
　　Plows the cleared land in valley and in lea,
Drives the hard wedge while crackling timbers yield,
　　Heaves the gnarled roots and leaves the woodland free.
Ennobling thought that ruled our Consul's breast,
　　Culled from his soul our Order's holy cause,
Retrieved the thoughtless from their wild unrest,
　　Upheld the good and framed the Woodmen's laws.
No ancient Woodman in the misty past
　　Left for our guide such pure or noble code—
We welcome all where'er their lot be cast;
　　Leave not the cottage for the rich abode.
Out o'er the States the Woodmen's Camp-fires glow;
　　Envy nor hate their onward march can stay,
Our *Echo's* notes in cheerful cadence flow
　　Noting the Woodmen's growth from day to day.
Dear to our hearts are those we learn to love;
　　Round failing Neighbors the Woodmen's arms are
　　　　twined
Made one in soul as through the world we move.
　　Onward we press, nor leave the weak behind.
E'en tho' black pebbles in our Urns be cast,
　　Our neighbor's cares shall be our own to bear,
Neglecting none; in future as in past
　　The good of all shall be our constant care.

Our aims are one, our heartfelt hopes combine
  Hope not for self but for our Neighbor's weal,
Fresh joys will rise when hearts with hearts entwine,
  Envy must die, and Love her powers reveal.
And every Camp-fire kindled to the wind
  A glowing tribute to our Consul pays;
Men yet unborn will mark his Master mind,
  Devoted Woodmen sing his deathless praise.
Erect an altar in the hearts of men,
  Cloak not the fact that Root, the truly good,
Reaps but his own, the wage of brain and pen,
  Our Order strong (but by his labor stood).
In him behold the Patriot and the Man,
  Nor cease your aid the Order to extend
Camp-fires ignite and do whate'er you can,
  Speed the good work, make Neighbors of each friend,
An Axe and Beetle and a Wedge provide,
  Uproot the Tares of Envy and of Pride,
  Let Woodcraft spread its blessings far and wide.

[This acrostic was written at the request of the publisher of the *Echo*,
the organ of the Modern American Woodmen, whose founder was Joseph
Cullen Root, who became its first Consul, to whom the poem was ascribed.]

[This poem was written in the city of London, in the year 1873, the motive being to show the serious and comic side of London life to the author's father, to whom he was writing, and in a facetious mood penned the poem as a letter.]

IN LONDON.

YOU think of coming up to town,
  The city of such great renown,
Where near four millions congregate,
From highest down to lowest state,
  In busy, bustling London.

Procure a map, ere you leave home —
Your destination be it known —
Peruse it well that you may trace
Thereon your destin'd lodging place,
  In busy, bustling London.

At Paddington you'll first arrive,
With cab and 'bus men all alive,
Honest some, but many a knave
Will strive your patronage to crave,
  And swindle you in London.

Now, if a cab or 'bus you take,
The charge first know, or bargain make,
Or they'll perhaps exceed their fare
And swindle when you are not aware —
  They do such things in London.

The miles, one hundred and a score,
A journey you ne'er faced before;
Midst change of air and change of scene,
Good appetite will intervene,
  When you arrive in London.

Here gaudy gin shops meet your view,
And reeking cook shops, not a few,
Real mysteries these of food and drink —
Before you use them stop and think
  Of what's consumed in London.

Prime veal that died before 'twas killed,
Mongst savory force meats here reveal'd,
And sausage rolls and Mobray pies,
Where, neath the crust, a mystery lies,
 In the public bars of London.

Your boots are dirty, make a stand,
A shoe-black's here at your command,
A penny is their legal charge;
And here an institution large
 Have these shoe-blacks in London.

But who they are none scarce can tell
Save that misfortune them befell,
And pity found them in the street
And took them to a safe retreat,
 The Boys' Refuge in London.

The victims of illegal lust,
Upon the world untimely thrust;
Or by their parents cruelly left,
As Arabs, living but by theft,
 Upon the streets of London.

But now reclaimed, they seek to give
Their labor for the means to live,
And they, some day, may prove to be
Good members of society,
 And citizens of London.

You've left your gardens far behind,
And country scenes to bear in mind,
Here comes a girl from whom you may
Procure a neatly-form'd bouquet—
 She's the flower girl of London.

Her slouching gait, disheveled hair,
Too plainly tell the want of care
That from a parent's heart should flow
To rescue her, fast sinking low
 In the labyrinths of London.

But charity and love stand by,
Who beckon, each with tearful eye,
And her frail compeers, day by day,
Are rescued from their downward way
    In black, vice-ridden London.

'Tis Sunday now ; we'll to St. Paul's,
Where every curious stranger calls,
Its unmatched architecture see
Displayed in massive masonry —
    The noblest work in London.

Here comes a gilded coach and four,
And coachman deck'd in lace galore,
The mayor of London sits within —
Midst all this pomp, he seeks his sin
    To wash away in London.

While some poor wretch without the gate,
Half conscious, looks upon the state
And pompous show the flunkeys play,
Who guide their master on his way
    When going to church in London.

What means this bustle in the crowd,
And voice vehement raised aloud,
And piteous whines as from a child,
That rises now in accents wild ?
    'Tis a beggar seized in London.

A mother and her starving boy,
Their time that morning did employ,
In selling matches or fusees
Their famish'd hunger to appease,
    Midst all this wealth in London.

And this is Christian liberty —
That proudly boasts that all are free,
Where men in church call each his brother,
But outside trample one another,
    And fight for place in London.

Through Cheapside on through Fenchurch street,
Where we the London Hebrews meet;
The Christian's Sabbath they ignore,
And trade and traffic with the poor
    In Petticoat Lane in London.

A stranger would not half believe,
Nor could his senses e'er conceive
The sights, if he should enter where
The Hebrews hold their Sunday fair
    In Petticoat Lane in London.

Here are clothes of every shape and make,
To suit the sober and the rake,
And gaudy ties and patent boots,
Or workmen's day and Sunday suits,
    In Petticoat Lane in London.

Anchors here at your command;
Coffins new and second-hand;
Dogs' houses, pigeon cotes and cages,
And literature of ancient sages,
    In Petticoat Lane in London.

Now let us take a two-penny 'bus,
Get on the top, nor make a fuss
If some foul fish-fag sit beside,
And claim the right with you to ride
    Along the streets of London.

We'll drive away to Rotten Row,
The two extremes of life to show,
For here is fashion on parade,
As if the world for it was made —
    The Upper Ten of London.

Flunkies here in powder'd hair,
Trim booted grooms without compare,
Their lords and ladies here attend,
Whose bearing none can comprehend
    Save those who've lived in London.

Here's many a dame in silks bedight,
Attended by a gallant knight,
Whose bearing doth at once unfold
The game he plays is but for gold,
    In Rotten Row in London.

The Serpentine here meets your view,
Where boating, fishing, skating, too,
Meet pleasures for the rich supply,
While poverty stands silent by,
    Midst all this wealth in London.

Your not being school'd to scenes like these
May bid you leave the boundaries
Where brainless wealth in wanton pride
From honest worth will turn aside,
    And snub you when in London.

From Hyde Park now, across St. James,
Where the queen in Buckingham Palace reigns,
By soldiers watched within and out,
Not daring e'er to walk about,
    In quietude in London.

Her servant girls and stable boys
May drink in London's mirth and joys;
A prisoner, she, midst gilded walls,
Subservient to the becks and calls
    Of toadying knaves in London.

The criminal lock'd in his cell,
At Millbank or at Clerkenwell,
Is not more guarded than the queen,
For rare indeed can she be seen
    By the populace of London.

From Birdcage walk through George's street,
Westminster Abbey we shall meet —
In cloistered crypts the shadows fall
On graven tablets that extol
    The dead of ancient London.

Some Cenotaphs were won by fame,
While others can but point the shame
Of regal prostitutes and kings,
That backward sad'ning memory brings
    Of wanton life in London.

But let's away from sights like these
And seek the heart and brain to please:
We'll go at once to Charing Cross,
Nor for the Horse Guards care a toss,
    But seek high art in London.

Trafalgar Square, by fountains graced,
Has at its head a gallery placed,
Where paintings on a hundred walls
The genius of the painter falls,
    To please progressive London.

THE CRY OF CONSCIENCE.

WHILE the thoughts of men are wandering,
    Calmly through the darken'd past,
  In the mazes of conjecture,
Listless of their shadows cast,
Listless to the cry of conscience,
    And the cravings of the soul,
Daring death, but ever trembling,
    Reasoning 'gainst the spirit's goal,
    And the power of God's control.

Judging others by their actions,
    As they feel so others must;
Only heedful of their longings,
    Never dare another trust.
Heaven to such is but a phantom,
    Naught to warrant a desire,
Naught to kindle love within them,
    Earth is all they can acquire.

May the spirits hover o'er thee,
    Kindling holy thoughts within;
O'er the quicksands of thy journey,
    Enter Heaven, freed from sin.
Reckless tho' thy early life-time,
    Near'd thee to the dark abyss,
Guarded from the Tempter's temptings,
    Inborn goodness won the bliss.
And to-day, in face of Heaven,
    Seek the right and wrong defy;
Never falter on life's pathway,
    Only seek a home on high—
    Ne'er to suffer, ne'er to die.

THE NATIONS' FAIR.

SEND your proud message through the world; Chicago
holds the Fair,
Nor keep her banner longer furled, but flaunt it to the air.
A tribute to her foster son, four hundred years denied;
Kings, queens and princes, one by one, reaped the spoils
for which he died.
Now let Colombo's honor'd name, on our city arms be shown;
Freedom demands his deathless fame, should be to the
nations known;
Then build a temple in the west and worship at his shrine,
And keep his memory in your breast who track'd this land
of thine.
A nation's hope born of his will — America the free;
In valley or on moss-grown hill; o'er plain or inland sea,
Columbus is our patron saint, if patron saint there be,
Rebellious hearts alone can taint the thought of such decree.
Let us a worthy mart prepare for the handiwork of man;
By one accord do each his share, do each whate'er you
can.
America's but yet a child, midst nations of the earth—
A nation born of toiling men whose prestige proves their
worth;
Unite in one accord to give a welcome e'en to kings,
Nor fear in foreign hearts to live, but seek their offerings;
Seek to unite the nations' minds in spite of caste or creeds;
Keep e'er in view the thought that binds, is a toiling
nation's needs.
Send out your couriers far and wide, and every heart en-
thrill,
And every man rise in his pride and show the nation's
will;
Our old friend, Santa Claus, will come with his load of soap
and toys,
Come boldly out from his winter home to greet his noble
boys:

And they in turn will welcome him for youth's remember'd
joys.
  Open at once your purses wide, and prove your native
    worth;
Prove that Chicago, in her pride, to the Nations' Fair gave
  birth.

THE HOME OF MY YOUTH.

FAR away in the valley the old cottage stands,
  With its rudely thatched roof and its moss covered
    caves;
Where the old ivy clings with its sinewy hands,
  And the jasamine twines round its time honored leaves.

'Twas there that the days of my childhood were spent;
  Where I roamed in the woods in the earliest spring,
To pluck the first violets that nature had sent,
  When with joy I leapt home the sweet trophy to bring.

It was there that I watch'd for the feathery throng,
  That throughout the dark winter had wander'd away.
When I drank in the music that flowed from their song,
  Till the nightingale's note would forbid me to stay.

How oft have I sat on the bank's mossy side,
  Till twilight her mantle had thrown o'er the scene;
When zephyrs, balm-laden, serenely would glide,
  And carry the cuckoo's note over the green.

No more can I gaze on such beauties as these;
  The cuckoo's weak note will not echo for me;
No more do the zephyrs soft fanning the trees
  Bear on the sweet music the songs of the free.

Oh, could I but choose from the city to roam,
  Where falsehood and crime overshadow the truth,
How gladly I'd turn to my dear village home,
  The thatch'd covered cottage which sheltered my youth.

A Mother's Dream of Hope of a Child
in Heaven.

MANY years have come and sped, many loved ones have
        departed,
And the cold world called thee dead, e'en the truly tender-
        hearted,
Round my heart thy love-light gleams as bright to-day as in
        the past,
Years of waiting are but dreams, from which I must awake
        at last.

Joys and sorrows here below are but the lights and shades of
        life
On the canvas moving slow, picturing scenes of love and
        strife,
Still the picture crowds my brain and fills my soul with calm
        delight,
Empyrean music's magic strain still cheers me on through
        nature's night ;
Parted but by God's decree, borne to realms of endless bliss,
Heavenly hosts awaited thee from out this sin-bound wilder-
        ness ;
Indian vestments once adorning thy fairy form with magic
        grace,
Now reflects thy young life's morning, again recalls thy
        heaven-lit face,
Earth restored thee in the dawning and with the seraphs
        found thy place.

Mary, when the Savior's voice echoes through the spheres for
        me,
Come and clasp thy hands in mine, lead me o'er the jasper
        sea,

Death is but a change of form, but our lives that form decide,
Upward then my beating heart seeks a home with thee to
    bide,
Fleeting breaths our cheeks are fanning here to-day, to-mor-
    row gone,
Friendship moves like meteors, through the star-depths on
    and on,
Enrapturing Hope now fills my soul and my heart still yearns
    for thee,
Ecstatic joys my vision sees when we shall meet eternally.

ACROSTIC TO TWO CHILDREN

OF MR. AND MRS. BRUSH OF CHICAGO.

LEAST and last of all the Brushes, bonny little Lynn,
    You to-day would play usurper and our loves would win ;
Nothing loth we give thee greeting, Hail thee! child of joy,
Not a heart throb less is beating for Baby Warren boy.

Both young souls are ours to cherish, both our cares will claim;
Round our hearts the love-tie lingers, ne'er to part again
Until Jesus bids you follow His immortal train.
Still our hopes would hold ye with us through our lives on earth,
Heavenward seeking rest eternal, in our second birth.

Buoyant Baby Warren, sweet roystering child of nature,
All the world's before thee, tho' listless of thy future.
But thy childhood rompings shall be like zephyrs moving
Yonder budding leaflets, nor friend nor foe reproving.

When winter's storms approach, or the summer's scorching sun
Attack thy young life's being, as the seasons onward run,
Repeating cares and joys may mingle peace and strife ;
Revokeless Truth will mark every moment of thy life.
Entered on the page of time, a candidate for fame,
Ne'er let thy acts nor words incline to mar thy kindred's name.

ETERNAL MARRIAGE.

JOSEPH from thy spirit home let me catch thy smile again;
  Even breathe me words of hope and thy conscious love
      maintain;
Out from Heaven's canopy watch thy young life's love once
      more.
  Unto her whose trust was thine when thou trod'st this
      earthly shore,
Send thy message in the morning, smooth her pillow when
      she sleeps;
  Note her heart-beats in the noonday, hear her prayer when
      twilight creeps.
Earth but claimed her for a purpose fix'd by God in His
      decree;
  In the nearing look'd for Heaven she again will cling to
      thee;
Place thy spirit hand upon her, bid her feel thy presence
      near;
  Calm the heart-throbs oft arising, bid her hope·and never
      fear;
Heaven's reunion soon must come, hearts and hands will join
      forever;
  Earthly duties being ended we shall live and love together;
Lock'd in Jesus' broad embrace nothing then our hearts can
      sever.

Mortal life was ever heaven since we trod the mountain side,
  Meeting in the Vermont valleys, wandering o'er the prairies
      wide,
City life with all its toiling found two hearts forever one;
  Cares and sorrows each dividing, each the other's will hath
      done.
Death his icy hand uplifted and it fell upon thy brow;
  Death to me will be my springtime, grant, oh! God, that
      time were now.

Under Saratoga's sod thou laidst thy toil worn body down;
    Unto Christ thy spirit fled when He claimed thee as His
        own.
Friends of thine and mine are round me, friends thine own
        heart made for me;
    Friends who wait the Saviour's summons from the earth to
        dwell with thee.
Fancy backward flies to girlhood when the world was all
        before us;
    Future then was but a shadow, hope and love a changing
        chorus;
Entering then on life's long battle, armor girded for the
        fight;
    Envy chasing cares o'ercoming, our only weapons truth
        and right;
Eternal love our only watchword and the Saviour's home our
        goal;
    Earth was but the marriage altar where we join'd our soul
        to soul.

SHADOWS—A REVERIE.

JOY took her seat in the halls of gladness,
   Love, Hope and Peace sat by her side,
Obtrusive Care with her veil of sadness
   Overtly came but to deride ;
Sweet Music, next, with her Orphean band,
   Urbanely sat with glistening eye—
Ecstatic sounds 'neath her tremulous hand
   Invoked her choir with symphony.
Pale Fear then approached with her silent tread,
   Softly behind the shadows came—
Heedless were they how their venom was spread,
   Enough that they knew of their bane.
Dear to our hearts are the memories of youth,
   Memories our souls will enthrall,
Ubiquitous spleen and sorrow, forsooth,
   E'en then our enjoyments will pall.
Repeated through life where'er we are found,
   Revilements that others have borne,
Are shadows that vex the poor and uncrown'd
   Remorseless of hearts that are torn.
Life is a meteor flashed through the spheres
   In *ignis-fatuus* shinings—
Darkened by shadows in youth and in years
   And bound by Sorrow's entwinings,
   Measuring its passage in tears.
Heaven's high attributes bind us to earth,
   Hope through its labyrinths twining—
A haven of rest, as measured by worth,
   Awaits on our soul's designing.
Venality binds in chains of despair
   Virtues, the nations are seeking—
Envy and Malice for truths never care,
   Each for itself ever speaking.
Nature that's vile plants in every breast
   Negations of justice to men—
Such are the shadows that make our unrest,
   Such was, and such will be again.

HEAVEN ON EARTH.

HAST thou pledged thy soul to God?
   Dost thou feel His love within?
Art thou by His guiding rod
   Fleeing from the paths of sin?
Truth and love around thee dwell ;
   Peaceful paths are thine to tread ;
Thine the joys of fate to tell,
   Out from sorrow's pathway led.
In the fitful paths of life,
   Ever ends the morning dawn ;
E'er with sudden changes rife,
   Nature's winding sheet is drawn.

Make thee, then, this life a heaven ;
   Be to thyself a constant law ;
And make thy modes of life the leaven,
   Forever holding God in awe.
Rest thee not from self's well doing ;
   Strive to leave a world behind
Inly better for thy wooing,
   Live to love and bless mankind.
And when earthly cares are ended,
   When the Father calls thee hence,
Nothing leave to be defended,
   'Gainst a heaven-won competence.

In this jealous world of mortals,
   Self is ever blind to woe ;
Crime bestrides the heavenly portals,
   Whence the sin-wash'd soul would go.
Health and peace and joy be given,
   Unto thee through life's long days ;
On thy head may songs of heaven,
   Ever spread their roundelays.
Live thy life on earth below,
   A spotless robe and crown to gain ;
Seraphic bliss thou then shalt know,
   Free'd from blighting mark of Cain.

THE LABORER'S APPEAL TO GOD.

GOD of Nations, let thy blessing
    Enter every home to-day;
Enter all the hearts of tyrants;
    Let their gold no more betray;
Onward, upward through the decades,
    Steel our hearts to brave the fight;
And vouchsafe us our belongings;
    In the battle for the right,
    Envy dim, and love enlight,
    Pour thy sunshine on our night.
Search the hearts of thoughtless traders,
    Speak thy power of truth to them;
Calm their passions, stay their venom,
    That would crush their fellow men;
Hope is dead among the masses;
    Every thought of peace is dying;
In our palace-burden'd cities,
    Vice and want are ever lying;
Long and weary hours of labor;
    Empty stoves and cupboards find;
Love and home is chill'd and darken'd;
    Nature seems accursed and blind;
Is it true, that thou hast power,
    Sorrowing hearts and souls to save?
Noting all the world's surroundings,
    When and what our natures crave;
Grant us then thy promised blessing,
    Ere we fill a pauper's grave.

TRIAL OF MEDICINE FOR THE ATTEMPTED HOMICIDE OF HUMANITAS.

PART FIRST.

Before their Honors, Chief Justice Ennui and Baron Skeptic.

COUNSEL FOR THE PROSECUTION—Professor Galvani Electrosis, Sergeant Voltas Magneticum and Doctor Abstemia Hydropathi.

The prisoner was defended by Hydrargyrum Allopathi, counsel to the Honorable Society of Annihilators, and Professor Herbarium Botanis, instructed by Alcobolsis Tobacium, legal adviser to the prisoner.

Libra Solidas Denarius watched the case on behalf of the County Commissioners.

The friends of the prisoner, feeling assured that the respectable position and the many services rendered to the community, among whom he had so long resided, would in this trying moment be all-sufficient in the eyes of an educated jury to warrant his dismissal and honorable discharge, they had, through his counsel, given the requisite notice for a "special jury." The following gentlemen were therefore empanelled:

1. HYDRARGYRUM CRETA.
2. PULVIS RHEI ET ZINGIBER.
3. TARAXICUM PODOPHYLLI.
4. VALERI ACONITUM.
5. AQUA MENTHÆ PULEGIUM.
6. BALSAMIUM BENZONI.
7. CAPSICUM ANNUM.
8. LOBELIA INFLATA.
9. CAPSUL PAPAVERIS.
10. INFUSIUM LUPULI COMPOSITUS.
11. VINUS SPIRITUS JUNIPERI.
12. EAU DE VIE FRANCAIS.

Their Honors, having intimated their readiness to hear counsel in the case, and the Crier having given the usual caution of silence, Professor Galvani Electrosis delivered his address for the prosecution.

ADDRESS FOR THE PROSECUTION.

M Y Lords and Gentlemen of the Jury :
     'Tis my most painful duty here to-day
To lay before you every circumstance
Of this man's crime and ultimate arrest.
The source from which our information comes
You'll find of such undoubted purity,
So free from every kind of prejudice,
That guilt will stand unveiled before your eyes.
And though the prisoner be one of those
Whose locks, now silver'd o'er with hoary age,
Have kept from all whose lives he daily sought
The secret of his most invidious will ;
The babe who, prattling on its mother's knee,

In all the roseate hues of infant blood,
Fell pale and wan where'er he forced his way,
And crept through life in healthless misery;
The schoolboy, bounding o'er the distant hill,
Unwary tript o'er some projecting rock,
When Medicine, with seeming kindness, called
On him to use his talismanic powers.
The scholar's friends to usage bent their wills,
And thus to custom gave what did belong
To Nature and her mystic potencies —
And aided thus this wily charlatan.
Start not, my Lords, at what I shall declare
Before those gentlemen into whose hands
The scales of justice shall a while be placed,
To watch the turning of the fickle beam,
I'll call before your Lordships and the Court
A dozen witnesses of this man's spleen;
Tear from his back the mantle of deceit,
And show how crime can live in genteel dress.
Yes, gentlemen, you and the Court will start
When witness after witness shall unveil
The prisoner's wily methods of deceit,
By which he led his trusting victims on.
They'll tell you how this man made desolate
The Hearths and Homes of thousands of our race,
To please the pampered few who hold the badge
And tack against their names the prized M. D.
I fain did hope, when first this brief I took,
That half the rumored charge was built on lies;
Nor ever dreamt one-third the crimes declared
Would find a pencil black enough to paint them.
All my forensic skill cannot but pale
Before the task my Client here hath set:
E'en though I stript the rainbow from the clouds,
I'd lack the colors of enormity;
For he, by many blandishments endow'd,
Hath oft deceived whole States and Governments,
And nations have been made by law to bow
Unto his will and blighted purposes.

And now, my Lord, tho' he hath 'scaped so long
And dared to live 'mongst people of repute,
The time has come when justice shall be done ;
And to that end I'll leave him in your hands.
In this, my opening speech, I aimed to be
As brief as would my subject well admit,
Knowing full well each witness would disclose
The long-kept secrets of this charlatan ;
At present I shall therefore say no more,
But call my witnesses before the court.

        *   *   *

GALVANI :   Call Tuberculous Hepatitis.

GALVANI :   You are Tuberculous Hepatitis?

TUBERCULOUS :   Yes, sir; that is the name by which
    I'm known
Among the members of the Faculty,
Who, for some reason, pledged themselves to keep
My name and character apart from those
Who have not paid for privileged consonants
Wherewith to form a tail-piece to their names.

CHIEF JUSTICE ENNUI :   You speak in riddles, sir !
    What mean you, pray?

TUBERCULOUS :   I beg, my Lord, your pardon if I do ;
But I have only followed in the wake
Of those who hold a license thus to call,
By names mysterious to the plebeian horde,
A common ailment known throughout the world —
And more's the pity, oft by ignorance bred ;
I am, my Lord, of whom you've often heard,
Inflamed, ulcerated liver.

LORD CHIEF JUSTICE ENNUI :   Go on.

GALVANI :   Now, tell their Lordships how you met
    this man ;
The conversation that you held with him,
And his reply and action in your house,
And all the effects of his first interview.

HEPATITIS :   My neighbor Lungs and I had fallen out,
And he accused me of obstructing him
In the discharge of his then occupation —
The taking to and fro of atmosphere.

HYDRARGYRUM :   I hold, my Lord, this is not evidence.
What have the quarrels of these men to do
With what is charged against my client here?
I hold this statement quite irrelevant ;
'Tis inconsistent with the laws regime ;
In fact, the leading up of evidence —

BARON SKEPTIC :   I think the witness should confine himself
To the indictment against the prisoner.

GALVANI :   I submit, my Lord, your Lordship's ruling,
And will guard my client in his answers.
Now, speak of nothing but what did occur
Between this man, the prisoner, and yourself.

HEPATITIS :   I told him the house in which I lived,
Had, from some cause unknown to self and friends,
Been so much shaken in the upper rooms,
That my best lodger, Heart, refused to pay
His usual tithe of labor for his home,
Which he ere now had done most willingly.
He looked around and felt each separate wall,
And with a seeming satisfaction viewed
The rents and tears that did disclose themselves,
And told me that he would send his workmen in.
I begg'd him not to detain me long,
For I did fear the fabric would succumb.
So shatter'd did it seem, I trembled much,
When Blood, "my servant," coursed along the rooms.
He told me of two workmen which he had,
Hydrargyrum and one Taraxicum,
And an apprentice named Podophylli.
These had, he said, of late been much employed
On shattered buildings, such as that of mine.
On this advice I bid him send them in,

That they the reparation might begin.
The workmen, when they came, I recognized
As having met them many a time before.
Even from my youth, Hydrargyrum I knew,
Who for companion then one Creta had ;
But, by the advice of one Botanis,
My parents did forbid his company ;
But thinking now that age had made him wise,
I bade him and his fellows use their skill.

VOLTA MAGNETICUM : But did you not apply for
  other aid in a dilemma of so grave a kind?

HEPATITIS : I did so to one named Allopath.
And to another named Electron.
But by the first's advice I did apply,
Much to my sorrow, to the defendant,
For since that time a number of my friends
Have sought the aid and proved the wondrous skill
Of one now known throughout the world —
I speak, my Lords, of him — Electron.

HYDRARGYRUM : My Lords ! I must protest 'gainst
  these remarks.
'Tis plain to see behind them rancoring spleen ;
Our duties here are but to hear the facts,
And truly gauge the measure of the charge.
This witness comes with prejudice enwrapt,
And only speaks like one who's sorely grieved ;
But e'en at this I would not now complain,
Provided he within the libel kept.
I hold, my Lords, the rules of evidence
Preclude such statements foreign to the charge.
I therefore hope my learned friend will see
The language of his client 's most inapt.

BARON SKEPTIC : The charge prefer'd against the
  prisoner
We see in the indictment clearly set.
Therein 'tis libeled that through ignorance,
Or the neglect of self or employes,

The prosecutor fell nigh unto death,
And but for timely aid must have succumbed
Unto the injuries that he thus received.
I therefore think, ere we can prove neglect,
It must be shown a knowledge possible
Among the members of the prisoner's craft,
And for that very reason I must hold
The witness justified in his remarks,
Wherein he did disclose the name of one
Who had prescribed unerring measures oft ;
And if it can be demonstrated here
That such was known unto the prisoner,
And that the knowledge of Electron
Had been disseminated through the trade,
Then he is clearly guilty of the charge.
The law is very clear in this respect,
As bearing on the crime of Homicide —
If any man shall by neglect convey
Or, knowing, cause to be conveyed within
A dwelling, building, place or covered way
A missile, compound, substance or machine,
Whereby the lives of the then occupants
Shall be in danger unto certain death,
Such person must within the law be held
As guilty of the crime of Homicide.

Volta Magneticum : My thanks, my Lord, for clear-
　　ing thus the way,
And sparing me the sorrow of rebuke
I had intended for my learned friend,
Whose interruption was unwarranted ;
But now, I hope my client will no more
Be interrupted in his evidence.

Hepatitis : These workmen told me that I need not
　　feel
The least alarm about my habitation.
They had, they said, discovered all the cause.
They said that Madame Bile, my housekeeper,
Had lately found my cook and kitchen maid

Remiss of duty in their work assigned,
And that while each the other did accuse
Of the neglect which led to this decay
Which showed itself around each stanchion's base,
And caused the joints and tie-beams to collapse
Until the king-posts, purloins and rafters fell,
And that one gable had at last succumb'd
Amongst the debris of the chamber.
My cook, Assimilative, I did call
And ask the reason of her negligence.
She straightway told me that Excremia,
The kitchen maid, had oftentimes been found
To throw her waste about the scullery floor,
Instead of through the drains assigned to it,
And hoped that therefore I would not deny
That in the preparation of my food
She 'd not be known to lack the trustful care
That should be e'er bestowed on Nature's gifts.
She did remind me how, in times gone by,
When I, much against her will, had ordered
A page named Alcohol to wait on me,
And how he did entice me with his condiments.
I bid her speak no more 'bout such as he,
For he, indeed, had caused me much unrest ;
But ere she left I asked her if she knew
How best I could proceed to remedy
That which had evidently been the cause
Of all my trouble and disquietude.
She told me of a cousin of her own,
Whose name was Chyle, a most industrious man,
My housekeeper, she said, had known him long ;
In fact, she many times assisted him
With means to carry on his operations,
And, when he last did call, he told Excremia
How buildings oft were ruined by the fact
That certain substances beclogged the drains,
Which, overflowing, injured every wall
And caused the building's premature decay.
He cited several instances in proof,

In which these substances were often found ;
Some noxious garbage filled with nicotine,
And rotten cereals charged with alcohol ;
But custom had so common made the act,
That Nature's natural drains were very oft
Into the veriest cesspools turned.
She told me that he did explain to her
How he had often coursed the conduit through,
And how the various channels did pour out
Into the vena portæ, as 'tis called,
So much of the chymificated mass,
Which from its very nature tends to build
And strengthens up the structure at its base,
In its mysterious but most natural way.
Her cousin's workmen, too, had suffered much
Through Excremia's carelessness and whims.
The brothers Lacteal, I think she said,
Were the names of these her cousin's employes
And, true to their employer's interest,
Refused their services to every one but he.
A number of reputed citizens
Had sought their aid as transports or as guides ;
But, feeling that the goods were contraband,
Unlawful and injurious to the State,
With true nobility of purpose stood
Against the tempting offers which they made.
'Mongst these was one Lupuli Infusium,
Who, from the magnitude of his estates
And manufactories of his various wares,
Had deemed himself all-powerful with these men :
But they did ever strenuously oppose
The introduction of his poisonous goods,
But, finding he was foiled in his attempt,
Sought out his neighbor, Dr. Allopath,
Knowing full well his most insidious power,
And how he held the kneeling multitude.
The doctor, feeling all his interests linked
With Lupuli and his friend Sir Alcohol,
Determined to attempt by secret means

To gain the service of the Lacteals,
And straightway introduced one Absinthi,
Whose comely mien and most engaging ways
Soon won the brothers Lacteal to their side,
Who did agree to take Absinthi through;
But they the treachery did discover soon.
E'en ere Absinthi crossed the outer hall,
His 'broidered cloak fell off upon the floor,
At once disclosing his true character.
They turned the traitor out, and since that time,
With wary foresight, all their aid refuse
To those who do not first their warrant bring,
And duly witnessed by their master Chyle.
Now, while she spoke, I did remember me
Somewhat about the circumstances she named,
For Madame Bile, alarmed, came to me
That I might send for some one to repair
The damage that the fellow then did do
To a partition in her ante-room.
Though simple as at first that fray did seem,
It caused us much confusion in the repair.
One Homœopath first sent his workmen in,
And, after working long upon the breach,
'Twas just as bad as when they first began.
The smallness of their tools when first they came
Provoked a smile from the porter in the hall,
Whose ready wit reverted to Defoe
And the great tribe of pigmies of Munchausen
In the now-noted land of Lilliput.
Botani then his sturdy fellows sent,
Who swill'd and plaster'd, drench'd and plugg'd the
        wall,
And by their noise my neighbors so disturbed,
That I would fain have kicked the fellows out,
While in material they were so profuse
That they did waste nine-tenths of what they brought,
Much to the injury of my furniture.
'Midst this confusion my friend Electron called,
And, seeing all the trouble I was in,

Did then a trusty tradesman recommend
Who late had risen into great repute,
Despite the prejudice of earlier times —
Had won his way to honor and to fame,
Until his magic name, Electron,
Had now become to all a household word.
I knew my friend Electron to possess
A most ingenious and a subtle mind
That e'en could penetrate the base of things.
He was, in fact, a true philosopher.
Nor was he one of those who dared to think
They had arrived at Nature's ultimatum,
And to possess the great panacea
For every want, and cure for every ill,
But did delight to own his ignorance
Of Nature's laws and subtle potencies.
In his discourse he'd often take one back
Into the past and distant centuries,
And show how much that every schoolboy now
Had set before him in his first primer
What to the savants of those ancient days
Was indissolvably mysterious.
I therefore told him that by his advice
I'd seek the service of the person named,
And when he left did send my messenger
And bade him haste and bring the tradesman back.
'Twas then the prisoner's son, named Calomel,
Did undertake the break to mend,
Ere I could gain an interview with him
My friend Electron recommended me ;
'Twas then that I did miss that good man's help,
Which might have aided me through other ills,
And have prevented most o' my present pain,
And all the troubles of this prosecution.
But the repairing of that damage done,
In which he gained my perfect confidence,
Was all the cause why I did call him in.
When the more serious damage did occur,
His workman. Hydrargyrum, took the charge

And guided in their acts the employes.
The work at first such progress did evince
That every day there seem'd a pleasant change,
When Hope, a long-lost friend of mine arrived,
Who joined with me and her companion, Joy,
In heaping praises on the prisoner's head
As being the architect of the repairs.
'Twas at this time my neighbor Lungs complained
Of my molesting him in his employ ;
But, knowing well that I had nothing done
In any way to injure him or his,
I straight demanded why he charged me thus
With an offence of which I nothing knew.
He said the workmen whom I had employed
Had cast their debris round about his home
And stopped the path o'er which his servant Air
Passed to and fro upon his messages ;
And, more than all, he said some poisonous stuff
That had been thrown upon his court-yard floor
Had mingled with the goods of which he'd charge,
And thus had cast discredit on his trade.
He said that even while he spoke to me
His halls and passages were so begrimed
With filth and dirt which from my dwelling came
That it so sickened him he'd scarce the power
To deliver himself of his complaint,
And that it pained him even then to speak.
I told him I was sorry thus to hear
A neighbor whom I had respected much
Make such complaint against my character,
By charges which I deemed most unjust.
I told him that a Builder I employed
Had sent his workmen in to do repairs,
And it must be they who did the acts
Of which he now so sorely did complain.
He asked me would I tell my Builder's name,
For he the charlatan would surely sue
Who dared assume so honorable a trade
And yet withal evince such ignorance.

I told him my Builder's name was Medicine,
And that he boasted of as fine a staff
As any among the members of his craft,
And did refer me to the institutes
That had conferred on him a merit badge
Which bore the names and the Director's seal,
And armed with this 'twas his delight to scorn
The propositions or the reasonings
That strangers to his craft should offer him,
Even though their brains were clearer than his own.
He'd boast the many dollars that were paid
Into the institutions where he lived,
And looked with such complaisance on the fact,
As though his gold could make a dullard wise.
My neighbor Lungs excused himself to me
For having been so harsh in his remarks,
And told me that he many times had heard
He had injured, through his ignorance,
Some of the finest buildings in the land.
But, not wishing to withhold the merit due
To an apprentice now in his employ,
Who certainly had proved himself to be
A far more skillful hand than Hydrargyrum,
And many now did praise the young Podophylli,
Who first was deemed a dull and clumsy lad,
But time had proved him skillful for his age
And worthy even now of some preferment ;
But that the aged Hydrargyrum had grown
Most past his usefulness to the State,
And should no longer stay in the employ
Of Builder nor of any architect ;
As on their skill there ever must depend
The wealth and being of the populace.
That man, no doubt, had served the purposes
And the requirements of an earlier age ;
But now the time had come when we should try
To superannuate him with his friends,
Lupuli and the elder Alcohol.
He told me that an aged friend of his,

German by extraction, but Anglicized,
Had trained his children, and his grandson, too,
Unto the honored trade of architect ;
And that the latter was no less a man
Than he whose name now stood on every tongue —
The famed, world-renowned Electron,
And who hath ne'er been known to fail in aught
That he had ever passed his word to do.
Among the many thousands that applied
To him as clients for his special aid,
He often hath been pained to tell the truth
That they their applications had delayed
Until the chances of perfect restoration
Would prove a difficulty and a task,
But even in a wreck of such a kind
Such a reparation he had often made
As to surprise the tenants and himself.

HYDRARGYRUM :   My Lords, I do submit most humbly
        to this Court
That nothing that this man's friend hath said
Had aught to do with what he here is charged.
Nor should your Lordships' nor our time be spent
In listening to this tirade of abuse
Against my client's most unblemished name ;
And even though we do admit the fact
That all is true, as by this witness told,
About the genius of the coming man,
Who hath lately so very much surprised
The honored members of the faculty,
That they each day are yielding to his skill,
And every hour are seeking to obtain
The privilege of an interview with him,
Who, with such rapid strides, rose up to fame,
And caused the wondrous name Electron
To be the password of a sure success.
That my client has his weakness, I admit,
In common with the best of citizens ;
But if we trace his glorious career,

And call to mind how kings and potentates
To him have bent the knee and homage paid,
And how each nation hath supported him
By tribute of their plants and minerals
Required to plenish each its edifice :
All this, my Lords, I think you'll see with me
Should have some weight in judging of his acts ;
And now I hope that the specific charge
Will straight at once be laid before the Court ;
Nor do I fear of the result, my Lords,
Left in the hands of this unbiased jury.

CHIEF JUSTICE ENNUI :   Will counsel please to state
    what witnesses
Are here subpœnaed in this case to-day,
And whether we had better not adjourn
Until the rising of the court below,
Which sits to-morrow by a special writ,
To hear the case adjourned from last assize
Of Vegetatus versus Bovine Alcohol.

MAGNETICUM :   We have, my Lords, some dozen wit-
    nesses,
But as their statements will be but to confirm
The evidence of the witness here in chief,
We think adjournment quite unnecessary.
Some men of science we shall have to call,
Who will explain how this man Medicine,
With recklessness and indifference,
Had been discovered many times before
In such attempts as now against him charged,
But that his name and purchased confidence
Had served to hush the charges brought against him.
Relying on my Lord the Baron's rule
Anent the question as to evidence,
I do submit that every issue should be raised
That has the slightest tendency to prove
The charge that here this Court has met to try.
And as evidence can only be
But of a purely circumstantial kind,

Which, by the way, hath by the law been held
To be the best and most reliable,
You gentlemen who are seated here to try
The issues of this complicated case,
Must not forget how clearly has been put
The Baron's ruling of the written law.
If we can by the evidence that's led
Demonstrate that the prisoner did know
And held at his disposal all the aid
Of that most valued man Electron,
And yet withal did so neglect the same
That my poor client came near unto death,
Then you, ere from that box shall turn to leave,
Must find him guilty of the charges led.

BOTANIS: I think, my Lords, my learned friend
    forgets,
In all the heat of his enthusiasm,
That we as yet have not approached the time
When he should take upon himself to charge
The jury with his own peculiar views ;
And since I've risen to correct my friend,
I would remind him what the witness said
About a person named Podophylli,
Which clearly proved the prisoner to be
A man who watched the progress of his trade,
And did his best at all times to improve
The less matured conceptions of his style ;
And we before your Lordships presently
Shall place such evidence as to rebut
The charges brought against our injured client ;
And we shall also show that he hath been
A most assiduous student of the styles
By men of studied tastes and great renown,
And has even lately seriously conferred
As to the forming of a partnership
With that young architect Electron.

COURT TOOK A RECESS OF 24 HOURS.

ABSTEMIA HYDROPATHI :   My Lords and Gentlemen,
    when last we met
You will remember how my learned friend
Did plead the prisoner's willing character
To try, and "e'en to hold in reverence,"
The plans and means of artists in his trade,
Who had outstripped the prejudice of time,
And dared to build on Reason's solid plans
In lieu of Fancy's ever-tottering styles.
While such admissions cannot but be praised
As bearing the undoubted evidence
Of one who felt the crushing weight of guilt
Was bearing heavily upon his soul —
Yet this repentance, while we praise it much,
Should nothing weigh in favor of the crime,
Which, undiscovered, might have caused the death
Of him who now, in spite of prejudice,
Dared here expose the prisoner's subtlety.
The witness Hepatitis now will tell
The conduct of the prisoner's employes,
And how one Aqua Pura rescued him
By timely action and the strong supports
He placed against the tottering edifice.

HEPATITIS :   My housekeeper, the Madame Bile, had
    made
An application for her holiday,
The which I granted, though reluctantly,
It being a season when I most required
Her supervision and discrepancy
In the beguiling of my menials —
For at this time the Misses Taste had call'd
And introduced a portly aunt of theirs,
The honor'd Lady Appetentia.
She told me that the distance to her home
Was but an easy drive, should I require
Her services upon emergency ;
That everyone within the neighborhood
Knew well her cottage by the Lake of Gall,

And that her neighbors bore her such respect
As to at all times seek out her commands,
And felt a pleasure in the serving her.
With this I did consent to let her go ;
But she had scarcely left the avenue
When all my servants in an uproar rose
And shook the very building while I lay
Encouched and helpless 'midst their rioting.
My lodger, Heart, now beat upon the floor,
And call'd my butler, Stomach, to his aid,
For he so trembled that he fain would sink
If some assistance were not rendered him.
'Twas then the prisoner sent in Alcohol,
Who had, he said, a special aptitude
In such disturbance as my lodger felt ;
So much so, that his very presence sooth'd
The violent tremblings of such violent men as he;
But for myself, he said that Hydrargyrum
As his helpmate, Flavia Chinchona,
Would best be suited for the work required,
Whose wide experience was to all men known ;
I noticed not their rough and heavy tread,
Along the Æsophagic Court and Hall,
But bid my butler watch the fellows well,
Or place his helper, Pepsine, in the charge
Of all the outer rooms and passages,
And sought the matron, Pancrea, to disclose ·
To me or him, if they should 'tempt to use
Materials of a rough or common kind
In the repairs about my dwelling house,
And from that time I do no more remember
Until I was awakened by my friend,
The aged Electron, who had hurried round
On hearing of the danger I was in,
And with him brought his friend—Electron
Of whom they told me that to him was due
The thanks and praise for my recovery ;
And there in his embrace I found myself
As I did 'wake to consciousness and life ;

—8

But as to the assault, I nothing know
Save that which I had from my butler heard,
Who told me each and every circumstance ;
How all my neighbors had become alarm'd —
While some did pity, the most did me abuse,
And look'd upon me as the head and front
Of the disaster that had spoiled their homes —
But I will call my butler 'fore the Court,
Who will explain each circumstance to you
As he before detailed them unto me,
And which determined me in this my suit.

CROSS-EXAMINATION.

BOTANIS : You told us that your dwelling long had
been
Subject to a crumbling and decay,
And that at other times you had been forced
To seek the aid of tradesmen to repair
The various portions of each separate room,
And that among them, one, Podophylli,
Had well succeeded in the patching up
Of a certain wall in an ancient room.
Now tell us how it comes about that you
Should charge the prisoner as being the cause
Of your prostration by the accident?
You nothing offer but the lame say-so's
Of idle, prattling, noisy employes ;
And, on the *ipse dixit* of their tales,
You dare to charge my client with a crime
Almost the highest on our statute books.
Just now you did admit you nothing knew,
Nor could you remember how the thing occurr'd,
And for your information did depend
Upon th' ravings of a frightened menial.
That there was some neglect none can deny,
And that you suffered much from the mishap,
But so far as my client is concerned,
You have not offered us one single fact

That bears the slightest implication on't.
Yet, if their Lordships and the Jury wish
To hear the witness whom you choose to call,
I'll offer no objection to the course,
As in a case of such a serious kind
There should be nothing stifled or held back ;
And for that reason I would gladly hear
Whate'er your witnesses may have to say.

BARON SKEPTIC :   There seems some hidden mystery
        in the act
Which caused the breaking up of this man's home ;
But whether 'twas the prisoner, Medicine,
Or any of his many employes,
Who did contribute to the accident,
Is more than we in this court can decide.
And though we did arraign the witnesses
Who here have come to speak unto the facts,
I cannot see that we should reach the end.
The prosecutor told most candidly
That he remembered little of the facts,
And though my aim hath ever been to sift
Whatever evidence before me comes,
Herein we have a case that must elude
Tho most searching scrutiny of the law ;
And for that reason now would like to hear
How think the Jury in the present case.
Now bid you, Gentlemen, your foreman speak.

EAU DE VIE FRANCAIS :   My Lords — My brother
        jurymen have listened through
The many charges brought against this man ;
And while we do deplore how much the prosecutor
Hath suffered through the certain negligence,
Yet we have long made up our minds to hold
The charge unproven as against this man,
We feel that our existence would be short, indeed,
But for the aid that he hath rendered us ;
For he so oft embellished our estates,
And did so decorate without and in

The many homes whereto we often go,
As to elude the ravages of time.
We do admit the cost is often great,
But that is nothing in the balance weighed
Against the crumbling of a cherished home ;
And if from among the subtle sciences
We can elect a member upon whom
We can depend in all emergencies,
We'll give the preference to such an one,
And throw aside our every prejudice :
And will proclaim unto the doubting world
The value of such wondrous services ;
But for the present we do think it well
That this inquiry for the present cease ;
For, in the absence of some stronger proof,
The verdict of our consciences must be,
And in which we all agree—" Not proven."

BARON SKEPTIC : I think the termination of this case
Cannot but give the greatest satisfaction
To one and all concerned in the inquiry ;
And will be by the outside world received
As certain evidence that justice sits
Free and untrammell'd in our ancient Court,
And for ourselves, we do congratulate
The gentlemen who with us were concern'd
In what did seem a complicated case.

VOLTA MAGNETICUM : We quite concur in all your
        Lordships say,
And thank you for your several courtesies,
While the prisoner, through his Counsel, thanks
The Prosecutor's friend, Electron,
As being the rescuer from what appeared
A certain issue unto violent death.

[The word "bobby" is a name given to the policemen of London by reason of the fact that it was Sir Robert Peel, the premier of England, who framed and passed a law to establish a body of men to take the place of the old watchmen, who were called Charleys. The passage of this law caused the people to rise as one against it, and to show a sense of opposition the cognomens "bobby" and "peeler" were applied to the men who became the first servants of the police system. It was in 1872 that the chief of the London police issued an order to vaccinate every policeman; hence the author composed the present song, which was sung at the time in the music halls of London.]

THE VACCINATED BOBBY.

COMIC SONG.

" YOU know there's been a mighty fuss
      This last six months or more,
About the vaccination act
      Imposed on rich and poor ;
The pros and cons of its effects
      Have caused a great disturbance,
And oft I've been a party to
      Enforce its strict observance.
Through courts and lanes, with book in hand,
      I felt myself elated,
When taking round the summonses
      To the unvaccinated ;
And round the squares I smiling left
      A notice in each lobby,
But then I was not what I am —
      A vaccinated bobby.

" I had heard of Jenner and his law
      About the vaccine virus,
And took for granted all they said,
      Though of its merits minus ;

But being myself an officer,
    Empowered by the State, sirs,
At anti-vaccination meetings oft
    Belabored many a pate, sirs.
Before his worship I have brought,
    On several occasions,
The parents who defied the law
    With whimsical evasions ;
Delighted in the court I've stood —
    These cases were my hobby ;
But then I was not what I am —
    A vaccinated bobby.

" One morning, posted in the hall
    Of every local station,
There was a notice headed thus :
    ' Police Vaccination.'
Each man was ordered to attend
    Next day before the surgeon ;
The whole instructions to relate
    Would need a second Spurgeon.
Next day we stood, with arms all bare,
    While each in turn submitted,
All laughing when the others winced
    When punctured and acquitted.
A nursemaid with three children came,
    All neat and plump and nobby,
To show the matter that was used
    To vaccinate the bobby.

" My turn was last, so I was left
    With children, nurse and baby ;
She look'd askance, and smiling said,
    " You are a timid gabey."
My arm being done, I summoned up
    Sufficient pluck to speak, sirs,
And enter'd freely into chat
    When we got in the street, sirs ;

She said she lived in Berkeley Square,
    And her master's name was Gobby,
And promised to accept the love
    Of the vaccinated bobby.

" The first three days I heeded not
    The punctures in my arm, sirs,
But on the fourth my cares began
    Which did me much alarm, sirs ;
My beat was round Trafalgar Square,
    St. Martin's and the Strand,
And opposite Northumberland House
    I often took my stand.
While I by Nelson's column stood,
    Unconscious quite of danger,
A lot of lads had gathered round
    A country-looking stranger.
A woman hanging on his arm
    Cried, 'John I'm sure they'll rob 'ee,'
And, for protection, seized the arm
    Of the vaccinated bobby.

" I moved them on as best I could,
    While I my anger stifled ;
But such misfortunes would, I'm sure,
    An angel's temper rifled ;
For the doctor bid me have a care
    To shield my arm from friction.
For if they broke before their time
    'Twould add to my affliction.
I hum'd a tune to lull my pain,
    Though 'twere not bass nor tenor ;
Just then I found myself beneath
    The monument of Jenner,
And looking up I silent sigh'd,
    And wished beneath the sod he
Had lain before the cause he'd been
    To vaccinate the bobby.

"The public who directions sought,
  My arm would oft times seize, sir;
So wonder not, I thought the cure
  Was worse than the disease, sir;
But all is past, and I am free
  From cares that prov'd a fetter.
And Mary Jane last night agreed
  To take me worse or better.
Her dowry is one hundred pounds—
  A maiden aunt bestows it;
So I my bargain don't regret;
  But quickly mean to close it.
She's given notice, sir, to quit
  The residence of Gobby,
And ask'd in church next week she'll be
  With the vaccinated bobby."

AN ACROSTIC.

[Written at Fresh Water Cave on the Isle of Wight. This Island is of great historic and geological interest, being a resort for invalids and tourists from the different parts of Great Britain.]

LOCATED on the sea-girt Wight
   The Eden planted Isle,
O'erspread with all that can delight,
   Or weary hours beguile.
Uplifted from Medina's bed
   Her mountain crests are seen ;
In every vale a carpet's spread
   Of never-dying green ;
Sweet Flora long hath held her court
   On Vecta's sunny shore,
And here her votaries resort
   And all their beauties store.
Shall we then sigh for foreign scenes,
   And leave this lovely spot ;
And brood for e'er o'er phantom dreams,
   Till lovely Wight's forgot?
Rome never could, in all her pride,
   Such beauties look upon ;
And Greece may set her groves aside
   With wasted Marathon.
Hesperian zephyrs 'round us glide
   With perfumes all our own ;
Joy, peace and hope are ever here
   Amidst the song bird's lay ;
Our terraced towns to mariner
   Give greeting every day.
Nor winter's blasts nor scorching sun
   Do our fair isle assail ;
Endanger'd seamen here may run
   Before the blinding gale,
Safe in our harbors find a home
   When other ports may fail.

COPPERS IN THE TRAIN.

[It is a common thing in London to find persons who earn a living by playing instruments in the separate carriages of London trains.]

"I'M a warehouse clerk in Watling Street,
    My duties are but small,
And my income's not affected,
    Though the stocks may rise or fall.
But I've been made unhappy
    By a girl to you I'll name,
It was Alice Wilhelmina, who play'd a concertina,
    And handed 'round her satchel
    For the coppers in the train.

"Though drearily the week goes 'round,
    On Saturdays I'm free,
To boat, or drive, or take a ride
    To Kew or Battersea.
From Moorgate Street to Pimlico
    I took a second class.
While waiting on the platform
    A voice said : 'May I pass?'
And the music of that sentence
    Did my heart at once inflame,
For 'twas Alice Wilhelmina, who play'd a concertina
    And handed 'round her satchel
    For the coppers in the train.

" When I got into a carriage
    She follow'd close behind ;
And when I offer'd her my hand
    Said she, ' You're very kind.'
Though her eyes were laughing mischief,
    They bound me by their spell,
And over head and ears in love
    At once with her I fell.

And when I courage found to ask
   The favor of her name, she said :
'It's Alice Wilhelmina, and I play a concertina,
   And hand 'round my satchel
   For the coppers in the train.'

"Astonished at her answer,
   I knew not what to say ;
But she unbag'd her instrument
   And quick began to play.
The charming music she discoursed,
   As she press'd the silvery keys,
Quite sent me off in raptures
   And the passengers did please ;
For soon I saw without a doubt,
   No novice at the game
Was this Alice Wilhelmina, who play'd her concertina,
   And handed 'round her satchel
   For the coppers in the train.

" Now, when I heard the coppers fall,
   Click, click, upon each other,
I quick began to reckon up
   One income with another.
Being somewhat quick at figures,
   As my business would imply,
A sum in mental 'rithmetic
   At once began to try.
Oh! I should like to marry,
   Was the thought that crossed my brain,
With Alice Wilhelmina, who play'd a concertina,
   And handed 'round her satchel
   For the coppers in the train.

" When I gave my contribution,
   I her hand did slyly press,
And whispered, as she sat her down,
   'Pray give me your address.'

She handed me an envelope,
  Addressed to Pickles square,
And said that any evening
  She'd be pleased to see me there.
I said 'I'd call,' and so I did,
  But the result I'll not explain,
Of my call on Wilhelmina, who played a concertina,
  And handed 'round her satchel
  For the coppers in the train.

REFORM.

WE want reform—
    In something more that politics or creeds;
We fain would see, humanity in man ;
For while the heart feels not a brother's love,
All measures fail to work their purposes.
Our greatest friends are they who do oppose
The whims and fancies we may hold,
For oft the truth may spring
From long engendered falsehood.

*   *   *   *   *   *   *

We want a church—
  Where selfish discontent may find its rest,
    Where one man's soul is not to others lost,
  Where every being will yield to Truth's behest,
    Nor seek preferment at another's cost.
  Where men shall feel that God is all in all,
    Where creedal differences can ne'er divide,
  Where every soul awaits the Master's call,
    When launched upon the universal tide
    Which bears us from the world.

An Enigma.

IF my first you would find pay attention, I pray,
 And note every object I place in your way.
Peramble the city or its environs at night—
You'll find it beneath the lamp's luminous light.
If you in the summer-time happen to dwell
In a village or hamlet, or even a dell,
Just notice the pastime of children in play;
You'll see how it's burden'd a part of the day—
How quiet it hath stood while they caper'd and swung,
'Tho' its back often creak'd with the weight on it hung

Of my second you'll find that Time is its king—
For the warrior brave it lowly will bring.
The youth or the maiden their beauty may boast,
But wrapt in its mantle their vanity's lost.

My third, tho' 'tis dumb, of great service hath been
To every class from peasant to queen;
Yet loud has it spoken, by figure and sign,
That a witness it's been through the era of Time.

I've dissected and shown you the parts of my frame,
Now I must leave you to find out my name.
Collect all my members and place them together—
You'll find me so small I'm as light as a feather.

THE LASS OF BOLTON MOOR.

THE LOVER'S RETURN.

O'ER Bolton Moor one morn I strayed
   To breathe its fragrant air,
When I espied a factory maid
   Most beautiful and fair.
No sandal'd shoes her feet adorn,
   No silken gown she wore ;
Yet she was bright as summer morn,
   The Lass of Bolton Moor.

Her wooden clogs with buckles gay,
   Shone bright before the sun ;
Her factory skirt of sombre grey,
   From coarsest fibers spun ;
The glinting sun-rays decked the dew
   Like spangled gem on mossy floor ;
With hurrying steps a-near me drew
   The Lass of Bolton Moor.

" Why so in haste ? " to her I cried,
   " 'Tis not yet time the bell to ring ! "
" To yonder mill " she quick replied,
   "I go without its summoning ;
I rise when others are asleep
   And seek to earn an extra store,
For I my widow'd mother keep,
   Because she's sick, and aged, and poor.

" That little mill upon the brow,
   Where flows the silvery stream along.
Is where I earn our living now,
   Yet 'twas our own in days a-gone ;

My father toil'd for many a year,
    And proudly watched his growing store,
When village lasses far and near,
    Worked in the Mill on Bolton Moor.

"That stream to me is dear as then
    When on its banks the flow'rets grew,
For well do I remember when
    We want, nor care, nor trouble knew.
But one sad winter changed the scene,
    When war his sad'ning message bore;
A cotton famine there was seen,
    Which closed the mill on Bolton Moor.

"The cotton lords their stocks with-held,
    And homeless thousands had to roam.
Then death my loving father felled
    And left us all without a home.
Mother and I, through many a year,
    Have kept the wolf from out our door,
But she is sick, and death is near,
    But I can work on Bolton Moor."

"Stay! maiden, stay! I've heard thee through!
    Retrace thy steps with me to go;
Thy sisters, and thy mother, too,
    Nor want nor shelter e'er shall know;
For I am rich, and thou hast won
    A heart that ne'er was won before.
Say, shall our hearts be linked as one,
    Sweet lass of Bolton Moor?"

"Thou art a stranger," she replied,
    "And yet, I feel thy soul is true;
For never since my father died
    Hath man so stirred my heart as you.
Give me thy name and I'll return
    With thee to mother's cottage door,
The story of my life to learn
    Since here we lived on Bolton Moor.

" While yet a child Lord Robert dwelt
    Behind yon frowning castle wall;
A proud disdain for each he felt,
    And played the tyrant over all.
Young Herbert was his youngest son,
    Who often walked beside the stream,
While lads and lasses, full of fun,
    Would sport and romp upon the green.

" But he, the son of haughty sire,
    Ne'er dared to join the village throng,
And thus in sadness would retire
    Midst mirth and joy and jocund song.
I knew his heart and felt the stings
    Of broken hopes within his breast,
Yet fruitless were our murmurings
    Against his father's stern behest.

" He told my father how he loved
    His daughter, I, the village maid,
And how his sire his love reproved,
    And how his banishment was laid.
From thence young Herbert ne'er was seen,
    And soon the proud Lord Robert died,
But never more beside the stream,
    Did Herbert walk at eventide.

" One night, beneath the castle wall,
    Four prancing horses restless stood,
When, from without the sombre hall,
    A listless figure slowly strode ;
'Twas Herbert, trembling in despair
    Against his parent's haughty pride,
For all his hopes were centered there —
    There was his home and hoped-for bride.

" The lackeys threw the coach doors wide,
    When Herbert slowly stepped within ;
His father, entering, sat beside,
    With venomed heart beclothed in sin.

They bore my love across the sea,
   Lord Robert died on Afric's shore,
And I was left as now you see,
   A factory girl on Bolton Moor.* "

" Forgive me, Mary, pray forgive,
   That I should force thee thus to tell
The cruel life that thou didst live,
   A life that I had known so well.
I am thy Herbert, I am he,
   Whom once a ruthless parent bore
To stranger lands across the sea
   From all I loved on Bolton Moor."

*Bolton Moor, Lancashire, England.

[The circumstances which led to the writing of this poem were as follows:
A person named Edwin Griffiths was superintendent of a Sunday-school and
teacher in the senior class, of which the author was a member. He on several
occasions had shown to his class-mates copies of poems he had written, and in
every instance where these poems were shown to the teacher, he had, without
exception, pronounced them copies of other authors. Therefore the author
wrote the following acrostic, being careful to withhold the fact that the initial
letters of each line, when combined, spelled the words "Edwin Griffiths."
When this poem was shown to him, he in his usual way exclaimed, "That is
not new; I have read it before." "I think," said he, "it was in the poetical
productions of Isaac Watts." When the author asked him if he thought Isaac
Watts knew him or his family, he said, "No." "Then is it not strange that
the name 'Edwin Griffiths' should appear in the lines?" This fact, when
pointed out to him, caused him to withdraw his statement, and ever after he
and the author were fast friends; and after thirty years had come and gone,
Edwin Griffiths, then an old man, remembered the circumstance only to point
out the moral, "that doubt and jealousy may become the parents of a lie."]

An Admonition.

EXTENDED forth from pole to pole, is Jesus' helping
    hand,
Dissuading all from sinful thoughts who join his holy band—
While we live on in worldly light with wealth our only care,
Ignorant of each coming hour or Death's grim lasting glare.
Not all the wealth the world can give will pay the debt of sin;
Granted alone in Jesus' name, forgiveness rests with Him.
Rise, sinner, now thy path renew, forsake the road to hell—
Inscribe thy mind with Holy Writ, that you above may dwell.
Fear not, though thorny be the way or dark it may appear—
Fresh sorrow will be daily found to keep thy heart in fear.
In true sincerity of soul, this day begin to pray,
That you be found at God's right hand when comes the judg-
    ment day.
How sad, when Gabriel's final trump shall sound the earthly
    knell,
Should you be faltering in your sin to bear the pangs of hell.

THE GREAT CONFERENCE OF BAGDAD.

AT WHICH THE DISCIPLES OF ALL THE HEALING ARTS WERE
REPRESENTED, IN THE YEAR 1890.

The following representatives of Medicine were present,
beside several other Sheolistic Professors from neighboring
cities:

HYDRARGERUM CUM-CRETA, President in the Chair,
SIMILIBUS CURANTUR, Secretary,   · · · ·
BROMIDIUM ALLOPATHI,   - - - - -
LILLIPUTIAN HOMŒOPATHI,   - - - - -   } All of Bagdad.
BELLADONNA BOTANISIS,   - - - - -
SULPHURA ARSENICUM,   · - - - - ·

Christos Galileum in behalf of the "Talmagian Society," had kindly offered the use of its rooms for the occasion, and in a neat little speech, opened the proceedings.

The choir, assisted by the Misses Faith, Hope and
Charity, sang with more than usual pathos, the beautiful
hymn: "Nearer, My God To Thee."

The Secretary having read the minutes of the previous
meeting, the Chairman called upon Christos Galileum, who
addressed the meeting as follows:

GENTLEMEN: I have the pleasure on behalf of our absent President, who is now fishing on the shores of Galilee
and Bethesda, or shooting around the hills of Capernaum,
while his son is playing "hookey" at the foot of Mount Sinai,
and his much devoted wife is founding a *Dorcas Society*
amid the distressed settlers on the banks of the *Dead Sea*,
to offer you the free use of these rooms, in the further-
ance of your holy cause, inasmuch as we feel that it is
"easier for a camel to go through the eye of a needle,
than for a rich man to enter the kingdom of heaven,"
therefore I feel that you, in your determinations, have
deemed it wise to people heaven with *poor souls* who

cannot pay your bills, and so give warm and comfortable quarters to the rich, who are willing to pay. If, therefore, at any time, myself and friend, the founder of our Society, can render you any assistance, you may always command us. [Much applause.]

CHAIRMAN: Gentlemen, I notice a stranger in our assembly, and I move that we at once expel him from this meeting.

CHORUS OF VOICES: Who is he? Who is he? Turn him out! Turn him out!

SIMILIBUS CURANTUR: Patience! Gentlemen, patience! I know the visitor; his name is Magneticum, and that he has proved his system just as my preceptor, Hahnemann, has proved his own against the opponents of former times. I, therefore move that he be allowed to join us in our deliberations.

SENSORIUM BOTANISIS: I second the motion.

CHAIRMAN: Gentlemen, you have heard the motion. Please signify your wishes by rising from your seats, so that we may count the votes.

BROMIDIUM ALLOPATHI: Mr. Chairman, before action be taken I submit that some inquiries should be made respecting this man, inasmuch as I am informed through one of his clients that he absolutely refuses to give medicine of any kind, and depends solely upon Nature and her potencies for his cures. Should we adopt such a system we would never be enabled to make a case!

I, therefore move that the motion be laid upon the table, and, moreover, I feel that our recently elected member, Homœopathi, should receive a vote of censure for his temerity in thus approving of this man's acts.

You all know that but for the coercive vote of the public, he, himself, would not now be here among us! As for Botanisis, the seconder of the motion, what do we know of him? Do not our wholesale drug friends of New York, Detroit,

Philadelphia, Boston and London, prepare for us all the herbs, roots and barks we require, and thus save us much time in the preparation of such trifling matters as making our own decoctions, pills, lotions, plasters, etc., etc., thus giving us more time to study the never failing effects of deadly drugs, which have in the past so helped us in our possessions?

The wholesale druggists, before referred to, can, as you know, supply us much more reasonably, as only cheap labor is employed in the manufacture of their compounds; and, besides, our neighbor, Coffinia, is enabled to aid us in our undertakings, and thus obliterate all evidence of our mishaps.

SULPHURA ARSENICUM: Mr. Chairman and friends, I am glad our worthy member, Hydrargerum, possessed the courage to thus dissent from the passage of such a motion. And I further submit, that Homœopathi be suspended pending an inquiry into his acts, for he, of late, with ignorance beset, near lost a limb of one poor townsman, and yet refused to settle his account by his exclusion from the public eye. You know, myself and friend, Hydrargerum, in such mishaps would not have left a trace of the mistake; while our much respected friend, Coffinia, would have gained a welcome fee, the lack of which he mourns; but, now, the murmurings of that poor man are through our city heard, and thus our foe, Discredit, casts his spleen on all our efforts!

'Twas only yesternight a messenger did call and told me of one of my clients who was stupid enough to live after I did three large doses give of soothing, sweet morphine! But there is at least some consolation in the fact that now the nether limbs are paralyzed for life, and thus, though the stubborn patient lives and not possessed of means to pay our bills, I know the house and lot must some time fall into our hands. For what is life on crooked sticks, with dangling limbs, withal? Yes! Gentlemen, herein we see a sample of our skill! We would, you know, a soothing course pursue, but, Nature's stubborn will will oft-times frustrate our attempts, yet, in the end, the profits are all our own!

PODOPHYLLUM MERCURIUM VEGETATIS :   Mr. Chairman, as a member of your learned Society, and even though a grand-son of your own, I do object to all this spleen ! You all remember when I was born, and watched my every day of life with interest intent, and must recall how many of you chided me, even in my infant years ; but you know the hold I have upon your hearts. My grand-sire and yourselves have, but of late, most seriously desired the superannuation of our most respected relative, and may we not in wisdom now admit our stranger friend, Magneticum ? For that reason I shall oppose the amendment of our friend Bromidium Allopathi and his seconder, Arsenicum, e'en though they oft have aided me in my efforts with my client Cutis, who was for years the attendant on my other client, Hepatitis Yet, they must remember many a strange circumstance, which, though perchance forgotten, may be recalled in mouldering bones beneath the granite laid. I fain would welcome here our stranger guest and greet him as a brother.

CHAIRMAN :   Gentlemen, were I not chairman of this meeting I would my guardianship forget !

Is it for this I raised this carping boy, Podophyllum, whose sire I sought 'midst vegetable growth ? I found him but a common tuber, o'ergrown with crude, misshapen, limb-like tendrils, and these the country Purgers would collect and use to physic all the bumpkins round, while some with canny witch-lore would describe the virtues of the mystic root, and so did coin a name to represent its form, and thus was first the common Mandrake known to members of the faculty, whose representative I was proud to be. We found that it did many virtues yield, such as to warrant our inquiry into its modes and actions on the human frame, and having thus discovered all the latent powers that long had lain unknown to men of skill and reputation, I, therefore, thought the young Podophyllum might some day take my place among the learned faculty. When from far distant Russia the thoughtful Paracelsus brought me and all my mercurial kin as guests among you, he little thought the reputation we should make, and win for him a never dying name. Therefore, it was for this that I did aim to keep the name of Mercury before the world—if not in riskful form as in the metal seen, we could at least amalgamate our race and yet retain the name, and so my elder daughter, Mercury, did the son of Mandrake wed, and thus their offspring in the boy Podophyllum you see, whose wild harangue hath caused me thus to speak, and should my daughter enter now and learn the perfidy of this reckless boy, her liquid, silvery face would blush for shame that her own son should thus disgrace his royal birth.

Where would our friends and proud associates attain the wherewithal their coaches to sustain, if nature should decide to strip our lineage from the book of time? I speak not now as chairman of your meeting here convened, but as the sorrowing grand-sire of my reckless kin, who, by his giddy thoughts and acts, would bring contempt on our most noble cause.

Gentlemen, forgive my seeming harsh harangue, for with a poisoning soul like mine a shattered nerve must needs evolve these tears. What say you, gentlemen, are your demands?

ANTIMONIALIS : Mr. Chairman and gentlemen, I have, in sorrow bent, listened to your arguments; well on in years and near to my demise, I fain would speak and all my soul pour out :

My master, Paracelsus, back in the centuries, lived among the heathen Turks, and with the monks immured in monasteries, did oft attend the sickening of their epigastrium cells, and this in spite of all the legal codes, did win his deathless fame. And he, I well remember, in his written books prescribed the ore magnetic in all its various forms ; and, 'neath his magic touch, the lepers rose and walked, and once more mingled with the tribes who had expelled them from their midst! I, therefore, feel the choler you evince may yet redound to your discredit among the thinking minds. I hope you will reflect upon the course you may pursue, or you, perchance, may seize the " business portion of a wasp," whose sting may leave a wound that even iodoform will scarcely

heal! Gentlemen, good night, and may reason all your
future measures lead!

CINCHONIA FLAVIA: Mr. Chairman, I, like my friend
the aged Antimonialis, have wept the while I listened to
your unseemly talk.

I do remember me, when, in the valleys of Peru, I
basked beneath the zephyrs of the setting sun.

A town was desolate, and fool M. D.'s did stand appalled,
whilst thousands kissed the dust and yielded up their spirits
to their gods.

A humble cow-herd, the sole support of his loved kin,
beneath a shattered roof and tottering stanchions lived, while
through the open panes, by native parchment filled, the sun
lit up the desolation of this crumbling home.

The then M. D.'s, pampered in their ignorance, did stand
and watch their weakening patients die. Now, by your per-
mission, I will tell the Faculty how my value was proclaimed.

The town was desolate and e'en the men of medicine did
die. The church bells ceased their evening calls to prayer.
The lamps, once hung from every open casement, now ceased
the shimmering of their flickering lights. The night-owls
mourned the company of men, while carrion vultures watched
from towering peaks the dying and the dead upon the stricken
plains! The God of Love, awakened by the call of his be-
trayed, did send his messenger into the homes of the distressed, who, panting for the liquid fuel of water from the
stream, did now direct the victims of the ever growing plague
into a seeming fœtid pool, at least one league away, wherein
a fallen tree submerged, beneath its face a slimy growth had
taken its abode. And this was all on which their hopes were
bound. Yet, they, like dying men "who grasp at straws," did
fill their pitchers from the fœtid pool, and homeward hied
them to their suffering kin. Soon as they sipped of its assuag-
ing draughts they found themselves from torturing fever's
curse to a life of happiness restored!

How great a panacea then was found, can best be told
in the pilgrimage of men who came from many leagues
around to pay homage to the man who thus did seem to be

a special instrument in the hands of God, raised up to show the arrogant pretenders to the healing arts how weak their claims to such preferment was.

Even the holy men, who self-immured in forest-buried monasteries, did hold a secret conference with the discoverer of the healing balm, and thus acquired its secrets and its rights. And hence the Jesuit's bark became an universal aid where'er its wondrous character was known. A shrewd and wealthy noblewoman attained the secret by costly purchase. The Countess Cinchon soon did spread its blessings o'er the land, and hence by chemic art our valued well-known remedy, quinine, is praised by all.

I thus have trespassed on your time only to show how seeming useless things may yet be recognized as an absolute necessity of our being, and warn you thus never to set aside or dare revile a thing of which you nothing know. Your holy calling, the healing art, demands your interests in everything that may present itself for your enquiry. The stupid, selfish acts of many of our older members who dared deride our much respected Hahnneman, whose wondrous insight into the potencies of the healing medicaments has built the homœopathic school and given us a set of men that must outstrip the clumsy dullards of an older age. A thousand similes like these could I advance, but I would fain retire and hear what other honored members have to say anent the question of admitting the applicant, Magneticum, as one of our most honorable associates.

Homœopathi : Mr. Chairman, I did not so soon after my admission to your honorable association expect so favorable recognition as that just given by our most respected member, Cinchonia Flavia, yet I felt it must be acquiesced in by you all. Nor do I blame the gentlemen who did insinuate that I did wrong in recommending the applicant, Magneticum, to membership. I know that he, like many of my friends, has so succeeded by his own peculiar means to bring from seeming death a number whom the members of our guild had left to die. I do admit the circumstance seems strange, but the strangeness of a fact should nothing weigh against the possibilities in other instances, that in our practices may at any time occur. Were it one single instance to which I do refer, it might be deemed a freak of nature—a mere coincidence—but when a thousand tests are made and result in like effect, I feel there must be some underlying law, not yet to us made plain, that may account for the seeming marvelous effects. And as our duties are as true Eclectics to recognize and hence encourage every man to honest purpose bent, who shall thus prove his value to the body politic, I do repeat my proposition, which was seconded by my friend Botanisis, and to make my motion in a clearer light appear, I here have penned the same in language most unmistakable, feeling assured that those who do not fear the truth will vote the motion aye. I would the Chairman read the motion.

CHAIRMAN : This seems to me a most unusual course and will, therefore, take the sense of the meeting ere I read the motion. What is your pleasure, gentlemen, shall I read or not ?

ALL THE MEETING : Read ! read ! read !

Moved, "That Magneticum Curantur, a citizen of Bag-dad, but lately domiciled, yet having demonstrated the value of his services to our State, be elected a member of our ancient Guild."

CHAIRMAN : The box is open, gentlemen, drop your ballot.

CHAIRMAN : Gentlemen, I find, on reference to your votes, that all save two have voted aye and, therefore, do declare Magneticum Curantur duly elected as member of our ancient Guild. I do regret that the two dissentents are my most respected friends ; in fact, I feel that but for them we should our meeting close, and all our practice would us nothing yield. Cigarus Tobacinus and Lupuli Alcoholsis have through three centuries been the patrons of our Art ; with-out their aid we never could have gained the competence we own, for health, in the place of varying disease, would

rule and what would our employment be if men were always
well.   As for myself, I nothing have to fear ; my time at
best must be short among you, yet I had hoped the mention
of my acts would long survive my presence with pleasing
memories, but now I feel that other scions of the healing
art will take my place, and I and all my works will be forgotten, save those wherein I did contribute to a mortal's
death.   I think, gentlemen, it is too late to offer the usual
prayer of thanks upon an election.   Though it to some may
seem abrupt, I do hereby declare our meeting closed, but
hope the members will reflect on their votes.   As for myself, I feel that we, to-night, have seen the nails into our
coffin driven.

COMPARISONS OF LIFE.

AS the bookcase is to the books, so is the body of man to
the soul.   The finely polished wood, the pleasing sym-
metry of its parts, the artistic carvings and its cunning
mechanism, hold close resemblance to the flesh and blood,
which mould into form and pleasing attractiveness, the veins,
the arteries, the bones, the muscles, and all their strange
concomitants, until the man, " the noblest work of God," presents itself for our admiration.   And yet, withal, this case of
living mechanism is but the crumbling casket of the deathless
spirit.   The books, themselves, clothed in all the gaudy
trappings of the binder's art, too oft conceal the spirit of the
speaking text ; and so the hidden characters of men are kept
from public gaze by gold-bought coverings and embellish-
ments.   A healthy body, above all worldly surroundings,
should be the aim and object of every living soul.   Such a
condition can only be attained by healthful exercise,
perfect sleep and a contented mind.   The glutton, nor the
drunkard, can ne'er attain to God's ultimatum — a perfect
man.

The curse of drunkenness, of all other vices, is the one

dread blot on God's or nature's constructiveness. The only animal that drinks intoxicating drinks is man, the only animal that abuses his God-made mechanism with tobacco is man and it is mainly the male portion of mankind who so demean themselves as to maintain the pernicious practice. What well bred man would like to go home from office, bank, factory or workshop, and find his wife and daughters sitting in parlor or dining room with pipes or cigars in their mouths, or slobbering a filthy bunch of tobacco between their teeth? If the habit of using tobacco is good for men, then why not for women? The male of all nations eat and drink the same form of food, whether liquid or solid, and therefore, by an honest parity of reasoning, it would be quite as right for the female as the male to thus make a sink-hole of the mouth and a smoke-stack of their nose. But, herein I feel my comparisons are odious, and therefore hope that we may never have to compare the human race with pigs, by teaching them to use tobacco instead of barley meal wherewith to give us our breakfast bacon charged with the vile perfume of nicotine. Neither would I wish to see a new industry manifest itself in the structure of female spittoons, nor bust pockets for female cigar cases and tobacco pouches; but if men continue the filthy habit, why not women? Should any lady of refinement now witness the vulgar habit as sometimes practiced by low women, it is only to make the comparison between the lady and the slouch.

WRITTEN AT THE TOMB

OF THE POET MONTGOMERY.

[This famous author was buried in Sheffield Cemetery, England.]

HE who once sung with pure poetic fire—
"Prayer is the soul's sincere desire,
Uttered or unexpressed,"
Here rests his weary head,
His soul from earth hath fled
To its eternal rest.

A silent prayer or psalm of praise
In soundless solitude may rise.
From buried crypts our songs may raise
An angel anthem through the skies.

'Tis not the sounding words alone
That reach the saving throne of grace ;
The parrot prayer will ne'er atone
For wrongs the heart will not erase.

The mind, the soul, the hidden sense,
The thinking, acting power within,
Can only claim deliverance,
Unburdened from its weight of sin.

Though tombs be built with massive walls,
And urns of gold may hold our dust,
The spirit leaves the sculptur'd halls,
And finds in God our only trust.

Then we should seek to leave behind
A more than crumbling marble tomb ;
Our aim should be to teach mankind
That ignorance seals a nation's doom.

Montgomery's dust lies here below,
　　While towers this shaft toward the skies ;
Yet songs seraphic ever flow,
　　To keep alive his memories.

'Tis not the cunning moulded stone
　　That wins us to his lifeless clay,
But 'tis his words, and they alone,
　　That thrill our hearts from day to day.

ADDRESS TO A LUMP OF COAL.

HAIL, ebon friend, all hail thy shapeless form!
The thoughtless minds know not thy hidden worth,
Which only see in thee thy light and fire—
Not knowing aught of the resources hid
Behind thy silent, unpretentious mien.

Only a lump of heat-producing fuel,
'But to be placed in stove or open grate—
There to diffuse its genial, pleasant warmth
And drive the blasts of winter from their homes.
This much of thee is all they seem to know.

A common shed—sometimes no shed at all—
Is all the care they would on thee bestow.
How few e'er think from whence or where thou cam'st,
Or 'tempt to trace thy ancient lineage
Through the æons of a long immured past.

And yet we know thou hold'st within thyself
A million years of heat-rays from the sun—
First stored in plants and then bequeath'd to thee—
And thence from thee to man—a thoughtless horde,
Who reap the fruit but reck not of its source.

We owe to thee the world's advancing arts,
Which give the poor the privileges of kings;
The horseless coach o'er trackless prairies speed,
While surging seas succumb to thy behests
When by thy heat, elastic steam 's evolved.

The factory walls, which mark the busy towns,
Owe most their growth to thy long hidden force
For ages stored by Nature's chemic art;
But when released it leaps with magic bound,
While wondering stands the gaping multitude.

They little dream that mighty trees had fallen,
And giant ferns, and sinewy climbing vines
Which held the oaks within their close embrace,
All fell into decay, and that from them
The life then changed is but revived in thee.

What of our homes, wert thou from earth divorced?
Our papered walls, our warm and wool-clothed floors,
Our furniture, and all the graceful forms
In fabrics seen, around our window panes
Which once by kings could only be attained :

The peasant class, the merchant's clothes may wear
And lab'rers' hours are shortened by thy aid,
While printed books the poorest may acquire
Which once alone, the wealthy could command
And even they, in meagre quantity.

The candle served the hermit and the squire,
While flickering lamps with smoky, noisome flames
Was all that lit the mansions of the great —
In fêtes or balls, or conferences of state,
Or led the devotee to church and prayer.

Thy liquid light, from oil or subtle air
Hath changed the scenes in trading marts and towns
Till sunlight seems none brighter than the rays
Thou dost evolve from seeming lightless stone,
To which the mass hath dared to liken thee.

For Tyrian dyes, of purple and of gold,
The merchant prince, his army would equip,
That they might gain by costly purchases
The much prized hue, for royal robes alone,
A color then, the poor dare not assume.

A veil of blue, and purple, and scarlet
Did Moses seek, the Ark to decorate;
And thus these tints through history hath been prized
In every land, by every nation sought
To influence all in their acquirement.

With spices rare, and fragrant costly oils
The nations sought, their persons to anoint.
But these were found in plant and shrub alone,
While months of toil some devotees would give
To gain a store, as offerings to their gods.

In modern times, ah! e'en to-day, we find
Our fashions yield to the same usages,
And the same hues which pleased the patriarchs
Or pride appeased among the courtly dames,
Yet now succumbs to fashion's vanities.

The perfumed clove, the bark of cinnamon,
The fragrant oil from almond nuts compressed,
And wintergreen their much prized odors yield.
All these are used by every class and kind,
Yet hitherto were sought from growing plants.

But chemists now can take the shapeless forms
Such as thine own—mere blocks of seeming stone—
Inodorous and tasteless as the air,
And out from these, by still and crucible,
Bring back the odors of the time-changed plants.

In our confections we oft these odors use—
Such as the clove, almond and wintergreen
And cinnamon—the oft-time tippler's pride,
Who seeks to hide a fetid, poisonous breath —
All these and more a lump of coal subscribes. .

The dainty miss may doubt the statements made,
But what of that? The truth cannot be changed;
And so would take the products close at hand,
Nor seek abroad for what we have at home
In thee, my friend, a grimy lump of coal.

A lady's glove, with city dirt begrimed,
A silken tie, some foppish beau hath worn,
If greasy spots should e'er on them be found
To benzine yields, no matter what the hue;
And this our friend the lump of coal provides.

Our household drains too oft offend our sense,
Or fever germs proclaim their deathly reign;
Carbolic fumes the mineral acid gives,
And thus ensure immunity from harm—
A lump of coal this wondrous acid yields.

A crimson ink and many purple dyes,
Magenta's charms from aniline appear,
And sun-lit tints, as from the Orient,
The dyer's art makes manifest to man;
Yet these we owe to thee—a lump of coal.

Thy nature still is but a hidden book—
We little know thy possibilities,
Yet fain would seek thy mysteries to unfold
And clearer make thy value to mankind,
Who now but know thee as a lump of coal.

I would describe thy every attribute,
But let a few suffice to make men think ;
Thy common claims to heat and light are known,
While there are those who dream not that thou art
A hidden source of joy and happiness.

Myriads of homes thy kin doth daily feed,
While trim built barks convey them o'er the seas;
The collier band—a happy crew are they—
With calloused hands and grimy faces, sing
The never-dying song—the lump of coal.

Thou oft hast stay'd the lifted hand of Death
When fell disease attack'd the homes of men;
Thy odors cleansed the putrefying air
While buoyant health usurped the place of pain,
And brought a peace from other source denied.

Benzole, benzine and oil of wintergreen,
And almond oil and pungent oil of cloves,
Sweet cinnamon, through thee, her oil doth yield,
Benzoic and carbolic acid hence
Their parentage to thee must ever own.

Herein we see the flora of a distant past
Locked in a case of blackest ebony,
Which only waits the chemist's magic touch
The long lost forest odors to restore,
Tho' seeming dead, can ne'er be said to die.

Adieu, strange source of known opposing powers—
Of sunlike rays and health destroying air,
Of deadly acids and balsamic aids,
All these to thee, "A Lump of Coal," we owe,
And thus a pæon to thy memory raise.

My Parrot and I.

MY wife and boys have gone
   And left us here alone —
    My parrot and I.
I've to cook my meals and make my bed,
And bring in the firewood from the shed ;
In place of rest we've to work instead.
But now no servant girl
At us her tongue can twirl ;
Yet in what we do, ourselves can please,
And if we would rest, can rest at ease,
There's none that ever attempt to tease.
One room is all we keep,
Wherein we eat and sleep —
    My parrot and I.

All the other rooms are locked and barred,
And my dogs without keep watch and ward,
While each for each is a constant guard ;
We sleep till break of day
And then we have our say.
If the day is fine we walk apace,
My shoulder then is my parrot's place,
And thus the streets of our city trace ;
Then in the busy crowd
We each are very proud,
And oft a curious glance is cast
By people who go hurrying past,
Of jokes we never hear the last —
    My parrot and I.

"MY SHOULDER, THEN, IS MY PARROT'S PLACE."

We visit all the stores,
Though we are counted bores ;
For it always happens when we're around
That a motley group of folks is found,
But we're philosophers, hale and sound ;
'Tis then we take our chance
At every face to glance.
All the male and female clerks await,
And watch my bird like a judge in state,
Till the floormen come and us berate.
Sometimes, perhaps, they will show us through,
And prate of their stocks "from Paris new,"
Which of course "we" know is seldom true —
  My parrot and I.

Some gloves of Lisle thread
Were on the counter spread ;
A flaming card o'er them supported
Announced that they were "just imported,"
While colors rare these gloves disported.
The weather being warm,
I thought 'twould be no harm
If I struck a bargain then and there,
And thus provide for the weather fair
When light gloves were wanted everywhere.
Then I looked them over pair by pair,
And sought the name of the maker there ; .
We found them a fraud and so declare —
  My parrot and I.

These quackeries of trade
In many stores are played.
You'll find that goods of every kind,
On the maker's hands are left behind,
And these in the cheap-jack stores you'll find,
With specious "ads" displayed.
These are the tricks of trade.

They may give the goods their proper name,
And truthfully say from whence they came,
That they are "job lots" they don't proclaim;
And so they lead astray
Their buyers every day.
'Twas thus they did betray
        My parrot and I.

Flannels are sold that never contain
One-half of the wool that you should obtain,
Though the price was named in language plain.
You are led to believe
That the goods you receive
Are all one wool, but are nothing more
Than stuff that is made for the notion store
And the Bon-Marchés, where frauds galore
The thousands will deceive,
And make dull folks believe
They are getting goods at half the price
If they'll buy just then through their advice;
It was just that way they did entice
        My parrot and I.

Since the fashion has grown
For a merchant to own
A variety store or a fair,
Where everything wanted is there,
From men's top boots to their children's wear,
Where candies, clocks and stoves,
And male and female hose,
And furniture, made to please the eye
Of inexperienced passers-by;
But for solid wear 'twere best to try
The men who make the goods
And understand the woods;
For shoddy we found in constant floods—
        My parrot and I.

In this whirligig age,
There are men who engage
In every form of traffic and trade ;
Dollars and dimes the custom hath made,
That men may each other's rights invade.
In dry goods stores we see
This strange monopoly :
Optical goods and crockery ware,
Tooth-brushes and brooms laid out with care,
With velvets and silks and laces rare,
Like the bumpkin's razor, " made to sell,"
Is the only tale these goods can tell.
We paid for this experience well—
        My parrot and I.

If common sense were used,
Men would not be abused
As they are now by the trader's tricks,
Who on shoddy goods large prices fix,
Then these reduce from twelve to six,
While 'round the town large bills are posted,
On which a marvelous sale is boasted,
Of damaged stock, by fire half roasted.
Sometimes we find that a bankrupt firm,
Whose name we now for the first time learn,
Has sold its stock to some great concern ;
This scheme we oft behold,
Though we were never sold—
        My parrot and I.

Our water-pipes were froze,
And at the winter's close,
We found beneath the kitchen floor
The store-room ceiling flooded o'er,
While my wife in sadness did deplore
The loss of her pickles and preserve,
And her candied fruits and sweet conserve,

Which she believed would the season serve.
But in this the plumbers were to blame,
For their work was not as they would claim,
As we found no drip-tap at the main.
But we, in language strong,
Denounced this crying wrong—
    My parrot and I.

These plumbers rule the town,
The laws are all their own ;
They do what they like and make their charge,
While on our neglects they will enlarge,
Then swamp our rooms like a leaky barge ;
And this they glory in,
Nor ever deem it sin.
If boilers burst in the kitchen range,
In which they had lately made a change,
They look in your face and say " 'tis strange !"
Such is their usual explanation,
This diamond shirt-stud generation ;
They are " you know " a queer creation,
    To my parrot and I.

They say " material's high,"
And look you in the eye ;
If you dispute the bill presented,
They say that you should be contented,
For nothing charged could be prevented.
Then the " wholesale " price list they will bring,
And prove to you that everything
Will always bear your examining ;
Then blandly ask if twenty per cent.
Is too much to charge for light and rent ?
But the discount sheet they ne'er present,
For there 'tis cut in two,
The price they show to you
    And my parrot and I.

We found that tricks of trade
In several stores were played,
And it seemed a never-changing rule,
With every chance they would befool,
But they always work it very cool.
The only check is our common sense,
Which we should use 'gainst each pretense
Of those who would offer dimes for pence.
No one can live on the cash they lose ;
Such logic our reason would abuse.
If thus " you are beat" there is no excuse.
But just take our advice,
And pay an honest price,
          As do my parrot and I.

Those men are beaten most
Who of their smartness boast.
Like a horseman who a horse would sell,
Is seldom found all the truth to tell ;
But with all their lies, they lie so well,
Each lie seems gospel truth,
Which battles every proof
That we may have against their dealing ;
For they evince such virtuous feeling,
That 'gainst their acts there's no appealing.
'Tis the horseman's methods that we see,
In every great community,
Where the sale and barter laws are free—
          So found my parrot and I.

We left the trading class,
In the Courts an hour to pass,
For there we were told that we should find
The Goddess of Justice, ever blind
To every act of all mankind ;
Where over the bench a sword is hung,
And the balanced scales are never swung

To the right or left for anyone.
'Twas a Justice Court — forgive the name —
For what we saw was a boodling game,
Where dollars and cents the verdicts claim,
And guilt went off "scot free,"
With which we couldn't agree,
    My parrot and I.

Justice, perhaps, may reign
Where higher courts disdain
To purchase and use the healing balm,
Too often sought by an itching palm,
When sensitive consciences may qualm;
While laws may be framed for all men's good,
The greed of gold too often hath stood
Sponsor for a Court's solicitude.
For those whose virtues are only wealth,
Which at best was gained by crime and stealth;
Such as worked for gold and "not for health."
We have known such men to rule a Court,
And laugh at Dame Justice in their sport,
    Which shock'd my parrot and I.

In a few short hours we saw
The farce of rendered law,
Where tardy Justice fell asleep,
While her scales their balance failed to keep,
And kept from jail all the blackest sheep.
We then the churches sought,
While upward rose the thought,
That there at least we the truth should find;
And so with these thoughts we charged our mind,
And every doubt we left behind.
With an humble mien and a solemn tread,
The aisles of the sacred piles did tread,
Then we took our seat, and bow'd our head,
    My parrot and I.

Of course we found some creeds
That could not meet our needs ;
But one great fact we were taught to know —
In whatever church we chanced to go,
That Charity and Love should flow.
Their creeds might differ, yet, in the main,
We found that the soul's all-reaching aim
Was but an eternal life to gain.
The liberal tongue where'er 'twas found
Would the Great Creator's powers resound.
Though the trackless depths without abound,
And though we have traced a world of crime,
'Twas leavened at last by God's design.

    Thus felt my parrot and I.

BOYHOOD GAMES.

I HAVE a family of boys
  That load me up with cares and joys ;
Yet they my happiness ne'er cloy,
    Nor break my peace of mind.
They leave their shoes in field or street,
And run about with naked feet,
While muddy legs they deem a treat
    That boys alone can find.

They never stay away from school,
I make for them that stringent rule —
In this they never me befool,
    As many boys will do.
But out of school they have their fun ;
With hoops and balls they're on the run,
And play their games till set of sun,
    With something ever new.

Of school-boy ethics ever proud —
This week 'tis tops alone allowed,
Their pockets then with whip-cord crowd,
    And every kind of string.
The cords that every package bind,
That to our house its way may find,
No matter what the size or kind,
    'Tis top-time's offering.

But all at once the game is changed,
The code of ethics must be 'ranged,
And tops at once must be estranged,
    For now 'tis marble time.

The early spring for tops may do,
But when the grass puts on its dew,
And buds and flowers the fields renew,
    And paths are free from grime,

Then out come "alleys," "glass" and "taws,"
"Stonies" and "clays" by marble laws
Are prized or shunn'd by sound or flaws,
    As by the rules appear.
Then round the corner down the lane,
Upon their knees they play their game
E'er watching for the mother's cane,
    If she perchance be near.

The ring is scratched, the pointers laid,
The forfeits that have to be paid,
By those who fail in promise made
    To reach the center ring,
Must be released to those who win,
And others soon their games begin,
And so on 'till there's nothing in
    The bags the losers bring.

"Now that ain't fair, you knuckle down,
That alley wasn't fairly thrown,
Your cheating can be plainly shown"—
    These are the words we hear,
When boys from school in marble-time
Describe their squares or pottle line
O'er which they make or lose the fine
    By usage rendered clear.

These boys will sometimes run about
With pockets fairly bulging out,
And raise aloud a merry shout,
    For they have stript the game
Of some unlucky skilless boy
Who might have been a parent's joy,
Who long-stored pennies did employ
    A marble stock to gain.

Then comes the kite for open field,
This is the game the fathers yield,
Their hearts against it ne'er is steel'd —
    This healthful exercise.
During the hours from shop or store,
The lath and bow they paper o'er,
And aerial flights in fancy soar,
    When kites before them rise.

The stick, the reel, the bobbin, too,
Wind and unwind the thread anew,
While bird-like to the cloud-land flew
    The buoyant, graceful kite.
But cruel fate would sometimes spread
Its venom to the kites o'erhead,
Which strike the tree or snap the thread
    Till all is ruin quite.

With bat and ball a legion games,
Bear in our sport such different names
Yet every nation ever claims
    Some game with bat and ball.
While some must face the bowler's aim,
Others a rising distance claim,
But every form a healthful game
    At once provides for all.

"Allrounders," "Golph" and "Cricket" now,
While "Rackets" seek the highest throw,
And "base-ball" craze is high and low
    In every state and town.
Ne'er let the games of childhood die,
But note the periods as they fly,
And store within your memory
    The games of old renown.

HOME.

MY wife had toiled for years,
  And borne with sorrow's tears,
    Ere fortune smiled.
We each the battle fought,
Nor care nor trouble sought,
Set jealousies at naught,
    Nor none beguiled.

We strove by word and deed
To meet each other's need,
    Our hopes to raise.
The malice of the world
Too oft at us was hurled,
But truth her flag unfurled
    And bless'd our days.

Our boys, a happy band,
None healthier in the land,
    Our heart's sole pride.
A world within themselves,
Yet, like the fairy elves,
In harmless mischief delve,
    But cares deride.

A plate for every friend;
Two hearts that e'er defend
    'Gainst want or woe.
The beggar at our door
Ne'er failed to share our store —
While affluent or poor,
    'Twas always so.

God, in his own wise way,
Will never lead astray
    The inly-good.
Though crimes may sometimes reign,
And look with proud disdain
On those whose honest brain
    For justice stood.

Mausoleums may be built
To hide the hidden guilt
        Of wicked men —
Men who the poor oppress'd,
And laughed at their distress
In heartless wantonness,
        Must live again—

But not in painted halls,
When retribution calls
        Their spirits hence.
But in unlooked for spheres,
Must live again their years,
And recompense with tears
        Their life's pretense.

'Tis not mere lip-address
That doth the soul express
        And worth maintain.
'Tis not the glibmouthed prayer
Oft uttered everywhere,
Feigned goodness to declare,
        Can peace attain.

Each soul its acts must guide
Responsive to the tide
        Where duty leads.
Then may we hope to own
A changeless Heavenly home,
Where sorrow ne'er is known
        To mar our needs.

We make our homes on earth,
The cradle of our birth,
        For future life.
We shape the paths we tread,
By crime or virtue led,
To homes of peace or dread,
        Or joy or strife.

FATHER HENNEPIN AT LAKE PEPIN, 1680. *Old Print.*

"Peering down on the busy encampment
That by magical swiftness was growing."

OO-LA-ITA.

A LEGEND OF MINNESOTA.

[A number of small lakes occur towards the sources of the Mississippi. *Lake Pepin* is an expansion of this mighty river, about one hundred miles below the Falls of St. Anthony. It has been very fully and beautifully described by Mr. Schoolcraft.

It is twenty-four miles in length, with a width of from two to four miles, and is indented with several bays, and prominent points, which serve to enhance the beauty of the prospect. On the east shore, there is a lofty range of limestone bluffs, which are much broken and crumbled, sometimes run into pyramidal peaks, and often present a character of the utmost sublimity. On the west, there is a high level prairie, covered with the most luxuriant growth of grass, and nearly destitute of forest trees. From this plain several conical hills ascend, which, at a distance, present the appearance of vast artificial mounds or pyramids, and it is difficult to reconcile their appearance with the general order of nature, by any other hypothesis. This lake is beautifully circumscribed by a broad beach of clean washed gravel, which often extends from the foot of the surrounding highlands, three or four hundred yards into the lake, forming gravelly points, upon which there is a delightful walk, and scalloping out the margin of the lake with the most pleasing irregularity. In walking along these, the eye is attracted by the various colors of the mineral gems, which are promiscuously scattered among the water-worn debris of granitic and other rocks, and the cornelian, agate and chalcedony, are met with at every step. The size of these gems is often as large as the egg of the partridge, and the transparency and beauty of color is only excelled by the choicest oriental specimens. There is no perceptible current in the lake, during calm weather, and the water partakes so little of the turbid character of the lower Mississippi, that objects can be distinctly seen through it, at the depth of eight or ten feet.

In passing through *Lake Pepin*, our interpreter pointed out to us a high precipice, on the east shore of the lake, from which an Indian girl, of the Sioux nation, had, many years ago, precipitated herself in a fit of disappointed love. She had given her heart, it appears, to a young chief of her own tribe, who was very much attached to her, but the alliance was opposed by her parents, who wished her to marry an old chief, renowned for his wisdom and influence in the nation. As the union was insisted upon, and no other way appearing to avoid it, she determined to sacrifice her life in preference to a violation of a former vow, and while the preparations for the marriage feast were going forward, left her father's cabin, without exciting suspicion, and before she could be overtaken threw herself from an awful precipice, and was instantly dashed to a thousand pieces. Such an instance of sentiment is rarely to be met with among barbarians, and should redeem the name of this noble-minded girl from oblivion. It was Oo-la-ita.

Father Hennepin was the first European who ever saw this lake. He reached it in 1680, and called it the "Lake of Tears," "because," says he, "the savages who took us, consulted in this place what they should do with

their prisoners; and those who were for murdering us, cried all the night
upon us, to oblige, by their tears, their companions to consent to our death.
Its waters are almost standing, the stream being hardly perceptible in the
middle."]

IT was up in the land of the waters,
   Where the silvery streams of Ouisconsin
Poured her floods to the proud Mississippi
Which roll'd on through the woods and the prairies
Till the rivers and seas were commingled.

There once lived in the vales of Keoxa
'Mong the tribe of the mighty Wapasha,
Oo-la-ita, the pure and undaunted,
The pride of the braves of the Dakotas,
The beloved of a daring young hunter.

I-ta-tomah the half-breed had won her,
Far away through the vales of Winona,
Where the wide-spreading walnuts and hemlocks
Overshadowed the Father of Waters
While in silence they row'd on its bosom.

Their canoes kept abreast in the shadows,
While their paddles kept time with the music
Which peal'd forth from their throats as they lingered,
And recounted their hopes and ambitions
When her parents should sanction their marriage.

They would anchor their crafts in the twilight,
Where, surrounded with red-berried brushwood,
They would sit 'till the lamps in the heavens
Lit the eddies that danced on the waters
That should tell them their time of departure.

Then the screech of the owl and the night hawk
And the buffalo's lowing was wafted
Through the trees up the wind soughing valley,
Which bore on its breath the barking of wolves
As they sped o'er the wide open prairie.

I-ta-tomah recounted his wanderings
Through the land of the Saukies and Foxes,
Where great Manitou's Isle in the waters
Holds the spirits of red men departed,
'Till the Father of Spirits shall call them.

Where their arrows no longer are leveled
At the braves and the foemen who wandered
In the quest of their stores for the wigwams,
Where the skins of the wolf and the panther
Are no longer required for their clothing.

He told of the treacherous Chippeways,
Of the home-loving, laboring Wyandots,
And the sly Winnebagos and Mandans
Who, through jealousy, fought the Dakotas,
Though they wander'd in peace through their valleys.

Oo-la-ita ne'er tired of his stories,
For her ears were e'er ready to listen
To the hairbreadth escapes of her lover,
From the arrows and tomahawks leveled
At his body through forest and jungle.

While the stars sent their beams through the branches
Of the trees that like network were woven,
The zephyrs would press with their fingers
The crisp sonorous leaves that were singing
The sweet love songs of hunter and maiden.   ·

While the shrill whip-poor-will in the distance
His monotonous story was telling,
The wildcat's growl rang out through the forest,
And the panther's scream, like beasts in terror,
Warned the lovers aback to their wigwams.

Now in their canoes, like swans on the water,
They each headed their way for the village,
While their crafts, soft and silent, moved onward,
And took up the refrain of the lovers
As their vesper notes rang on the air.

But, alas, came the hour of their parting,
When her eyes peering out from their casements,
Seem'd to gleam with the starlight of heaven,
And lit up the bronzed face of the hunter
As she nestled her chin on his bosom.

When he bade her good-night at the wigwam
Of her parents who had waited her coming,
He dream'd not of the fate that hung o'er her
When he went to his lodge on the border
Of the stream where their love boats were anchored.

Tho' the wigwam was gladsome with music
That re-echo'd its sounds o'er the water
As they struck the high banks of the river,
He knew not of the boisterous rejoicing
Which rung out in continuous laughter.

I-ta-tomah that night on his blanket,
In his lodge on the banks of the river,
Kept awake, for some reason he knew not,
For his soul was at peace with his fellows—
Now his love, Oo-la-ita, would wed him.

In his snatches of sleep he would see her
With her bow and her quiver of arrows,
And the pelt of a panther around her,
While the broad spreading plumes of an eagle
All betold of her valor and prowess.

In his dreams of the near coming future,
He would picture her riding beside him,
Reining in her fleet steed while they tarried
To take aim at some beast of the forest,
In the height of her woman's ambition.

Then he rose with the sun in the morning,
All gladdened with the hopes he had woven
In his wooing the fair Oo-la-ita,
The pride of the Sioux and Dakotas,
And the kin of the mighty Wapasha.

Tho' he felt that the blood of the white man
Had long cast on his race its dishonor,
Yet he pointed with pride that Zumbrota,
The foe of the Padoucas and Mandans,
Had married his mother, Minneiska.

As the waters of fair Minnehaha
Seemed to dance in their glee through the valley,
Till they fell o'er the falls of the Zumbro,
And together flowed on with the streamlets
Till embraced by the Father of Waters.

It was thus that the brave I-ta-tomah
Did picture his beloved Oo-la-ita,
And would sing of their loves and their longings
Until each, in undying embraces,
Should go home to the Father of Spirits.

With the steel and the punk-wood he kindled
The lodge fire for his meal in the morning;
And when back from his chase through the thicket,
A young roe was thrown over his shoulder,
The feast he had promised Oo-la-ita.

Then he waited till weary of waiting,
While untouched was the meal he'd prepared her;
But he knew not the cause of her absence,
Though he felt she would never deceive him,
For they plighted their troth to the spirits. .

In his anguish he went to the river
And released his canoe from its moorings;
Through the lilies and lotus he paddled
Till the sun had crept up to its zenith,
While half conscious, half dreaming, he waited.

Then he heard 'round the bend in the river
The wild voices of braves through the forests,
While the musical notes of the maidens
Was borne on o'er the breeze with its perfumes
Which betold of some maiden's betrothal.

Here I-ta-tomah pensively waited
Till a squadron of boats were upon him,
Each being loaded with stores for a journey,
While the head of the party was Redwing
With his squaw, the once peerless Waseca.

They, the parents of fair Oo-la-ita,
With Ne-noth-tu, a brave of the Mandans,
Who with Redwing routed the Chippeways
When they sought to destroy the Dakotas
And usurp all the lands of their fathers.

'Twas for this that Waseca and Redwing
Had long promised their daughter in marriage ;
'Though the war path nor chase he could follow
Ne-noth-tu with wisdom and influence
Could subdue every foe of his friends.

All the village had formed a procession,
And had loaded their boats for the journey
To the Lakes where they gathered their pigments*
For their war-paints and festive surroundings,
This a custom the tribe always followed.

It was thus that this season of gladness
Was plan'd for Oo-la-ita's betrothal ;
All her brothers and sisters agreeing
That she owed them her sanction to marry
Ne-noth-tu, their friend and protector.

They had chosen the broad Lake of Pepin,
Where her heart and her hand should be given,
And 'twas there that the tribe were advancing
When I-ta-tomah watched from an inlet
His beloved Oo-la-ita row by him.

---

* NOTE—It was an annual custom for the tribes to meet and gather the
blue clay and other pigments which were found on the banks of Lake Pepin.
These were used for war paint and other purposes.

Then he plan'd to continue his journey
To wherever his loved one was taken,
And determined to die, or to win her,
But his life should be dear in the purchase—
Thus swore he to the God of the hunter.

All the village seemed floating before him—
The young braves and their laughing young lovers,
And each squaw to her papoose was singing,
While they paddled their boats through the lilies
Which now burdened the air with their perfume.

Ah-la-ah-quoi, the star of the village,
With Ki-sah-thoi, the light of the wigwams,
Glided merrily on o'er the waters;
Oo-la-ita, their sister, between them—
Three maidens, the pride of the Dakotas.

Then Mi-was-ha, Oo-la-ita's young brother,
With a squaw of the tribe of the Shawnees,
Who had come with a brave and a trapper
Far away from the land of Tecumseh,
On the breast of the Father of Waters.

They were here as the friends of Ne-noth-tu,
To witness his long promised nuptials
With Oo-la-ita, the pride of the wild wood,
On the banks of the lake and the river
Where the tribes seek their pigments each season.

With Ne-noth-tu was Shas-ka, the elder,
And best loved of Oo-la-ita's brave brothers;
The warrior was dressed in his trappings,
In which he had routed the Chippeways
When they came to the lands of Wapasha.

His moccasins of dress'd mountain goat skins,
Of the same was his shirt and his leggins,
And all fringed with the scalp locks of his foes
He had slain in his young days of battle
When he fought for his tribe of the Mandans.

Though his hair had grown white with his prestige,
His long white waving tresses were mounted
With a band of the skins of the ermine,
Pierced around with the quills of the eagle,
Interlaced with the shells of the rivers.

O'er his shoulder his bow and his quiver,
That had carried the death-dealing arrow
To the brave who had faced him in battle,
Or the trapper who roamed through the forests
Killing off the wild beasts of the red men.

They had built them a raft for the freighting
Of the poles and the skins for their wigwams,
While they dwelt on the banks of the waters,
Where they hoped for a long festive season
When Oo-la-ita should marry Ne-noth-tu.

Then I-ta-tomah watched from the inlet
Till the last of the rowers pass'd by him,
When he loosened his boat from its moorings,
Which he deftly threw over his shoulder
With his bow and his quiver of arrows.

Well he knew of the tribe's destination,
And determined to reach there before them ;
Then he plan'd a straight line through the forest,
Thus avoiding the tortuous windings
Which the river had cut through the valleys.

Thus he traveled all day until sunset,
When again he came up with the river,
Where he camp'd for the night by its waters ;
Then he wove him a duck-trap of willows,
And in silence laid down on his blanket.

Ere the sun had bedeck'd the horizon
With its bright streams of crimson and gold,
Or the meadow-lark rose from the grasses
The earth-worm for its nestlings to gather,
Or the fly-catcher flew from the brushwood,

I-ta-tomah gathered the tamarack,
And had lit him a fire for his cooking
The wild duck he had trapped in the willows,
And the herbs he had pick'd near the streamlet,
Which in silence flow'd down to the river.

When the meal of the morning was finished
He walk'd down with his boat to the river,
Then he deftly row'd out on the waters
While he pointed his course to the northward
Far ahead of the band of Wapasha.

A thick network of lilies and lotus
Formed a serious stay to his progress,
But his muscle and nerve never faltered
For he knew that his foes were behind him
With his loved one in utter subjection.

Yet the winds seem'd to blow in compassion,
For it bore on its wings of the morning
The loud songs of the braves and the maidens
Who were merrily skimming the waters
Which would lead to the lake on the river.

Oo-la-ita dreamt not that her lover
Was preceding her tribe up the valley,
And was listening the while to the voices
That rang out on the winds in the morning
And which told him how near was their presence.

But this was the sole thought that consoled him
And astringed all the force of his muscles
As he pull'd his fleet craft o'er the waters,
Being determined to double the distance
'Tween himself and his foes now behind him.

So that night on the waters of Pepin,
In a cave hidden deep in the thicket,
Away back from the gaze of the rowers,
He tied up the good craft that had brought him,
And then waited the dawn of the morrow.

Then he made him a meal of the berries
While he sought out a spot for seclusion,
There to rest and to wait for the morning
When Wapasha his braves would assemble
And the squaws fix the poles for their wigwams.

Soon a wide-spreading oak he discovered
Away down a ravine through the brushwood,
Where a rock, with its towering summits,
Hid the streamers of light to the westward,
When the sun sank to rest o'er the hilltops.

Here he laid himself down in his blanket,
His medicine-bag bound to his body—
This the skin of a beautiful ermine
He had caught when his dreams in his boyhood
Bade him gather his medicine early.*

Then I-ta-tomah made this his totem,
Which he placed on his blanket and clothing,
And when hunting, wherever he traveled
On the tree-bark, or stone, it was pictured,
That his friends might know where he had journey'd.

All that night he was restless and thoughtful,
Save the moments of slumber he gathered,
But in these he was burdened with visions
Of his loved one, the fair Oo-la-ita,
Who knew not of his efforts to save her.

Ere Aurora her couch had forsaken,
I-ta-tomah was pacing the valley,
When his ears caught the echo of voices
Which the wind bore away through the branches
And warned him the tribe were assembling.

---

*When a Dakota Sioux or Mandan Indian boy was fourteen or fifteen years of age, he was sent to the woods to find his medicine. He made a couch of boughs and then lay down without food or drink for several days, the power of the medicine bag being in proportion to the length of the fast. He would afterwards accept death rather than part with his medicine bag.

Then he climbed up the perilous pathway,
Which led up o'er the rock on the river ;
And when he had surmounted the summit
He laid down in the tall mountain grasses
That grew there in luxuriant splendor.

It was this coign of vantage that gave him
A full sight of the country around him ;
Yet not one of the party below him
E'er conceived of the watcher above them
On the rock towering up to the Heavens.

He look'd down on the braves as they landed
All the tent-poles and skins of their wigwams,
And the squaws hurried 'round in confusion
While locating their place of encampment
For the feasts and the sports of the season.

The long practiced eye of I-ta-tomah,
Through the years he had wandered the forest,
Stood him well in the strange situation
The events of the day had now brought him,
Which demanded the sight of an eagle.

From the precipice where he was sheltered,
His keen vision was spread o'er the prairies,
And he watched in the distance the coming
Of peaceable tribes of the Indians,
Each the crystals and pigments to gather.

He looked down on a patchwork of color,
Like a quilt of gigantic dimensions,
Deeply fringed and entasselled with brushwood
Which the edible berries emblazoned
Like the gems on the robe of a monarch.

But the lake was as still as at zero ;
Not a ripple was seen on its bosom,
Yet the rays of the sun glinting downwards
Shaped its surface in numberless facets,
Like a diamond, fresh from the cutter.

While deep down on its pebbly bottom
The cornelian and agate and onyx
And chalcedony lay with the granite,
Which, far back in the ages unnumbered,
Formed the peak of a towering mountain.

Mountain Island stood out in the distance
Like a giant on guard at the entrance
Of the lake, where the proud Mississippi
With the waters of Pepin commingled
In their silent and peaceful embraces.

On the rock that tradition has christened*
Oo-la-ita looked up in amazement,
As she caught the strained glance of her lover,
Peering down on the busy encampment
That by magical swiftness was growing.

All the Chiefs their war-whistles had hidden,
But the rattles and drums and deerskin flutes,
And the mystery whistles were blowing,
Which betold of the Dog Feast† preparing,
Every tribe, in their friendship, to welcome.

The canoes, in broad squadrons, were floating
Far away to all points of the compass,
While the rattle of hoofs on the prairies
Bore their sounds on the air o'er the waters
Where the tribes had prepared for their feasting.

But the silent and sad Oo-la-ita
Sought the woods in the guise of a huntress,
And then leaped like a roe o'er the hillocks
Till the rock's craggy summit was conquered,
Where she fell on I-ta-tomah's bosom.

---

* See illustration.

† The chief pledge of affection among these tribes was the Dog Feast.
When we consider that no where on the face of the earth is the dog so valued
as among the Indians, therefore the sacrifice of their dogs is the strongest
evidence of friendship.

There they lingered, their love tales recounting,
Till the sun had crept up to its zenith,
Then they parted to meet in the valley
When the curtain of night had dropped o'er it,
That they then in the silence might wander.

Each determined to cling to the other,
And appealed to the Father of Spirits
To protect them o'er mountain or prairie,
Or wherever their steps might be guided
In their flight from their cruel oppressors.

To the beach Oo-la-ita descended
Where she met all her sisters and brothers,
And her father and mother and kindred,
With the aged Ne-noth-tu, her suitor,
Who had sought her their marriage to hasten.

They each reasoned in vain her agreeing,
Then they threatened to force her obeyance,
But her womanly pride was resistless,
For her heart she had pledged to another—
I-ta-tomah—the loved of her childhood.

With her bow and her well plenished quiver
She stood out in defiance before them,
And dared them to force her to marry
The old Chief against whom all her nature
From her childhood had ever revolted.

"You tell me you love me! Is this your love ?
To force me to wed the brave I despise,
Chain my young life to the foe of my soul,
And chase from our home the brave of my heart,
Who hath faced every danger for me ?

"Then you say you're my father and mother,
And my sisters and kindred and brothers,
But tho' I have told you I love not the brave,
Yet you would mingle my blood with his tribe,
While my I-ta-tomah wanders alone.

"If this be your love, I'll bid ye farewell,
Nor sister, nor daughter, nor kindred I'll be,
For I know the Great Father will guide me
To the Home of the braves and my loved one,
Where in spirit we'll live on forever."

Like a steed from its tether she bounded,
And then leaped to the rocks like a panther,
While in wild consternation her brothers
Were as speechless as mutes in their terror,
For they knew Oo-la-ita's intentions.

From an o'erhanging crag on the mountain,
She looked down on her kin and pursuers,
But in vain they attempted to reach her,
While she held them at bay and defied them
Like a Baron secure in his fortress.

Should they climb to the ledge where she halted,
They all felt she would jump to destruction,
So they calmly stood back in their terror,
And attempted to reason and win her,
While in stolid defiance she listened.

'Midst the tumult of voices uprising,
Every echo rang back in confusion,
And as snow melts away in the sunshine,
So their words on the ether were wasted,
And by gesture alone could they reason.

Then she swept round the trees to the summit,
Looking out o'er the circling horizon
When I-ta-tomah rush'd to embrace her,
Like a vine to the oak she entwined him,
As they calmly look'd out o'er the landscape.

Now the sun in its liquid effulgence
Lit the faces of maiden and hunter
As they gazed on the Heavens above them,
While their arms were outstretched as appealing
To their God for protection and succor.

MAIDEN ROCK, OR LOVER'S LEAP.   *Old Print.*

" But the spirits of maiden and hunter
Are oft seen round the shores of Lake Pepin."

From behind came the clamor of voices,
Then they turned, but to see their pursuers,
Old Ne-noth-tu and Shaska, her brother,
And Redwing, her father, approaching,
Their arrows at I-ta-tomah leveled.

As quick as a flash of the lightning,
Brave I-ta-tomah's bow was unbended,
And an arrow flew out from his fingers
Which pierced the cruel heart of Ne-noth-tu,
Who was driving to death Oo-la-ita.

When Zumbrota, I-ta-tomah's father,
Had fallen at the hands of Ne-noth-tu,
The young brave swore a bitter avenging,
And 'twas here in the presence of Heaven
That the fates forced his foe to subjection.

Now the arms of the hunter and maiden
Were each lock'd in the other's embraces,
And e'er brother or father could save them
They had leaped to the life never ending,
In the spiritual home of the hunter.

But the spirits of hunter and maiden
Are oft seen round the shores of Lake Pepin,
Each collecting the gems from the pebbles
As mementos of earth and its sorrows,
When with mortals they mingled and suffered.

THE ONLY TRUE HISTORY, LIFE AND ADVENTURES OF PALLAS ATHENA.

TOLD FOR THE FIRST TIME IN KANSAS CITY.*
1892.

ATHENA'S PAPA SWALLOWING HER MAMMA.

While Cronus and Rhea were afloat on the air,
  They dump'd down on Olympus three wonderful sons:
The oldest was Hades, a wild, devil-may-care,
  Who in underground caverns his government runs.
The next was Poseidon, who now rules o'er the seas,
  While the daughters of Nereus float over the waves.
In their salt water home they all live at their ease,
  Far away from divorce courts, in coral-built caves.
But Zeus, the younger and mightiest of all,
  Overpowered his brothers and put them to flight,
And out from the darkness he Aurora did call,
  Who gave to the world all the blessings of light.

---

*For several years the merchants of Kansas City have held a pageant
every October, Pallas Athena being the tutelary goddess represented.

SURGICAL OPERATION BY HEPHÆSTION, M. D.

Now young Zeus was one of the boys in his days,
    Like the young Prince of Wales among Britons to-day ;
For the daughters of Earth he was seized with a craze,
    From his home on Olympus he often would stray ;
Sometimes as an ant, or an eagle, or spider,
    He would come down to Earth in the search of his prey,
And thus his dominions were made much the wider,
    While his wife stay'd at home and had nothing to say.
His wife was named Metis, who was once a schoolmarm,
    But she was so exacting his life to enthrall ;
Yet her brain mathematic made learning a charm,
    And he cheerfully swallowed her, school books and all.

THE BIRTH OF ATHENA.

Old Hephæstion had watched from his smithy hard by
    The wild cannibal act of the truculent god ;
So he pick'd up his ax, his chastisement to try,
    And then laid him out flat as a flail on the sod ;
Zeus sprang to his feet in a terrible rage,
    Tho' his skull it was split from his nose to his ears ;
While in deep contemplation his mind did engage.
    From his wife, now digested, Athena appears.
The maiden, Athena, spread her arms in delight,
    And when once from the skull of her father was free,
Said she, "My dear papa, I will hurry my flight,
    And bring to Olympus a solace for thee."

ATHENA VISITS KANSAS CITY.

Far away from the East and Olympian heights,
    On the steeds of the Zephyr, Athena now came
To the land of Columbia, the home of delights,
    With her father's commission, the solace to claim :
Then backward she hied to the crags of her birth,
    Where she found her papa nearly maddened with pain ;
But her panacea, of measureless worth,
    Soon restored the split skull to vigor again.
It was thus that Athena and Zeus, her sire,
    Did determine forever to visit the West,
Where the children of Earth perfect homes could acquire,
    Thus grew Kansas City at Athena's behest.

ZEUS MADE WHOLE.

And Zeus, now heal'd, stays at home with his daughter
    Ten months in the year, with her Priests at her side,
But, as in the past, to our city they brought her;
    These Priests in the future will still be her guide.
Yet we think 'twould be well, in her journey next year,
    To bring Hades and Poseidon here on a float,
For Poseidon our waterworks jumble might clear,
    And our board of works boodlers seek regions remote.
Then heigh-ho! for Hades and Poseidon, the brave,
    Come on with Athena, when she visits the West;
Bid the waterworks crew in their mud-puddles lave,
    And the cable car fiends, yield the people's behest.

Elect honest men and give each a backbone,
　　And a strong arm to down all the boodling crew;
Make the whole board of works their shortcomings atone,
　　Rule again our fair city with methods anew;
Let us light up our city with means that are sure,
　　Nor burden our taxpayers, nor let them go free;
But be just to all classes, the rich and the poor, ·
　　Then a prosperous city our city will be;
Let our alleys be cleared of their garbage and filth,
　　And cable slots gauged, as the charters demand;
Our city will then be renowned for its health,
　　And Pallas Athena be queen of the land.

SPIRITUALISM AND CREEDS.

LISTEN to the tramp of angels, heed their words of calm
    reproof;
They are treading 'neath your portals, they are watching o'er
    your roof.
While the creedists tell of Moses, speaking face to face with
    God,
While they mark the rush of waters yielding to his magic
    rod;
While they tell of Abraham's greeting to the angels in his
    tent;
Of Elijah's fiery voyage, and the spirit voices sent
Through the burning bush to Moses, and to Balaam through
    his beast—
These are facts they all rely on, from the greatest to the least;
But if we hold our communion with the friends gone on
    before,
They are ready to denounce us—they would strike us to the
    core;
They would tell us it is Satan playing off his arts on men,
Or that there's some dispensation that hath changed God's
    laws since then.
They would have us look on Nature, changeful as their shallow
    minds;
Point us to eternal greatness, just as veering as the winds;
Tell us of a God repentant, of the works His will performs;
Tell us of a God of mercy, yielding vengeance through the
    storms—
Storms of fire and brimstone dealing, o'er the hearths and
    homes of men,
Gloating o'er the fallen weak ones with a more than fiendish
    ken:
This, they say, is true religion—this the picture of their God,
Who, with Adam, walk'd in Eden; who can alter with his nod
All the laws as known through Nature—all the actions of
    our life;
He, they say, can curse or prosper, He can yield us peace or
    strife;
But our spirit friends are with us—aiding us our journey
    through;
Dear, departed friends are round us, ever hopeful, ever true,

And they tell us of their journey, how they met the friends
 they loved,
How the frail ones are progressing, and how fruitless creeds
 had proved.
It was not the God of creedists that had led them through
 the spheres,
Nor can creedal hell-fiends bind them in the so-called vale of
 tears,
But the ever bright effulgence from the upper spheres descend-
 ing,
Is the beacon guiding onward, thither are their footsteps tend-
 ing;
There the spirits, render'd perfect, dwell in everlasting bliss;
But they know not of the Great One, more in that life than in
 this;
Nor the creed of Athanasius, which would lower God to man.
God incarnate—thoughtless blunder—taught as a Creator's
 plan.
They would have us and our children all their creedal love
 believe,
In a God with carnal passion, such the pure can ne'er conceive,
And, if we sign not their charter, if we reason or inquire,
Then they meet us with damnation, scourge us with eternal
 fire.
Then they give their God location and a visionary throne,
With a parliament around him, members of their sect alone.
When the sunbeams strike too fiercely, when the rain-clouds
 hang too long,
When some princely head shall sicken, then their prayers are
 fervent, strong;
Then they ask their God unchanging just to listen to their cry,
Just for once to change His purpose, and their selfish wish
 supply.
Creedal teachers preach of mercy, while their dogs are better
 fed
Than the toilers on your highways while they seek in vain
 for bread.
But listen to the spirits' story — they tell not of sects nor
 creeds,
But they point to halls of brightness where progressive good-
 ness leads;
They tell not our erring brothers of an unconsuming fire,
But would lead them through life's portal, onward, upward,
 ever higher.

General Index.

www.ingramcontent.com/pod-product-compliance
Lightning Source LLC
Chambersburg PA
CBHW020626030726
47497CB00007B/2429